MAB JONES

and the

DOOMSDAY BOOK

Will Mabbitt writes. He writes in cafes, on trains, on the toilet and sometimes, when his laptop runs out of power, he writes in his head. He lives with his family somewhere in the south of England.

Ross Collins grew up with an affinity for drawing, the bionic man and precariously swinging backwards on chairs. Finding it hard to make a career from either of the latter two, he continued drawing and has since written and illustrated many award-winning books. Ross resides in Glasgow, Scotland.

MABEL JONES and the DOOMSDAY BOOK

By WILL MABBITT
Illustrated by ROSS COLLINS

PUFFIN

PUFFIN BOOKS

UK | USA | Canada | Ireland | Australia
India | New Zealand | South Africa

Puffin Books is part of the Penguin Random House group of companies
whose addresses can be found at global.penguinrandomhouse.com.

www.penguin.co.uk
www.puffin.co.uk
www.ladybird.co.uk

First published 2017
001

Text design by Mandy Norman
Printed in Great Britain by Clays Ltd, St Ives plc

A CIP catalogue record for this book is available from the British Library

ISBN: 978-0-141-36293-9

All correspondence to:
Puffin Books
Penguin Random House Children's
80 Strand, London WC2R 0RL

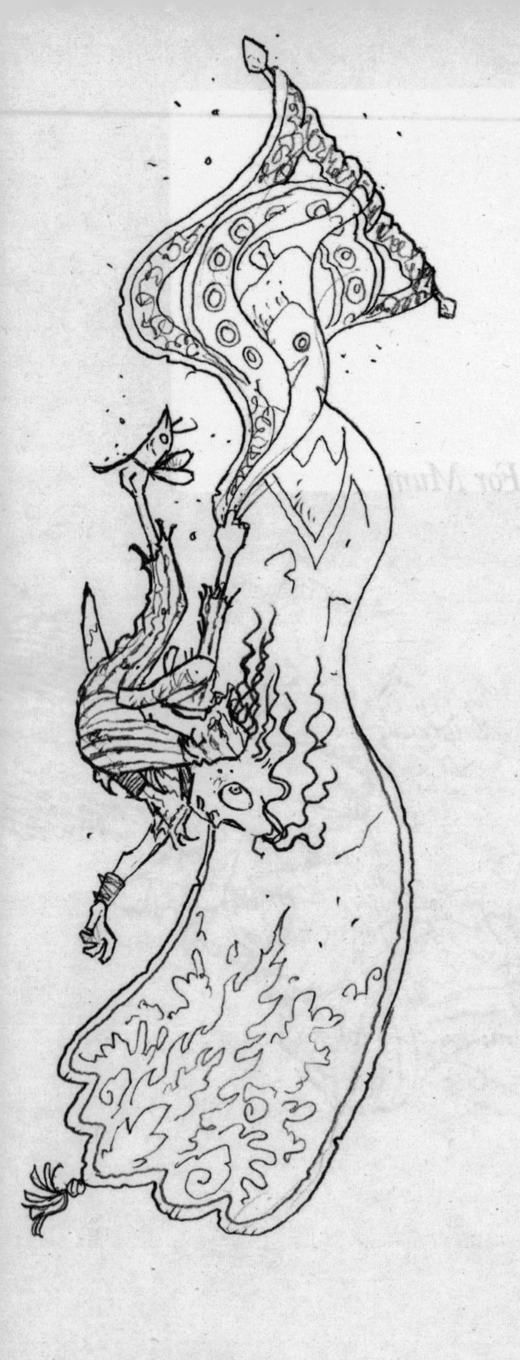

CONTENTS

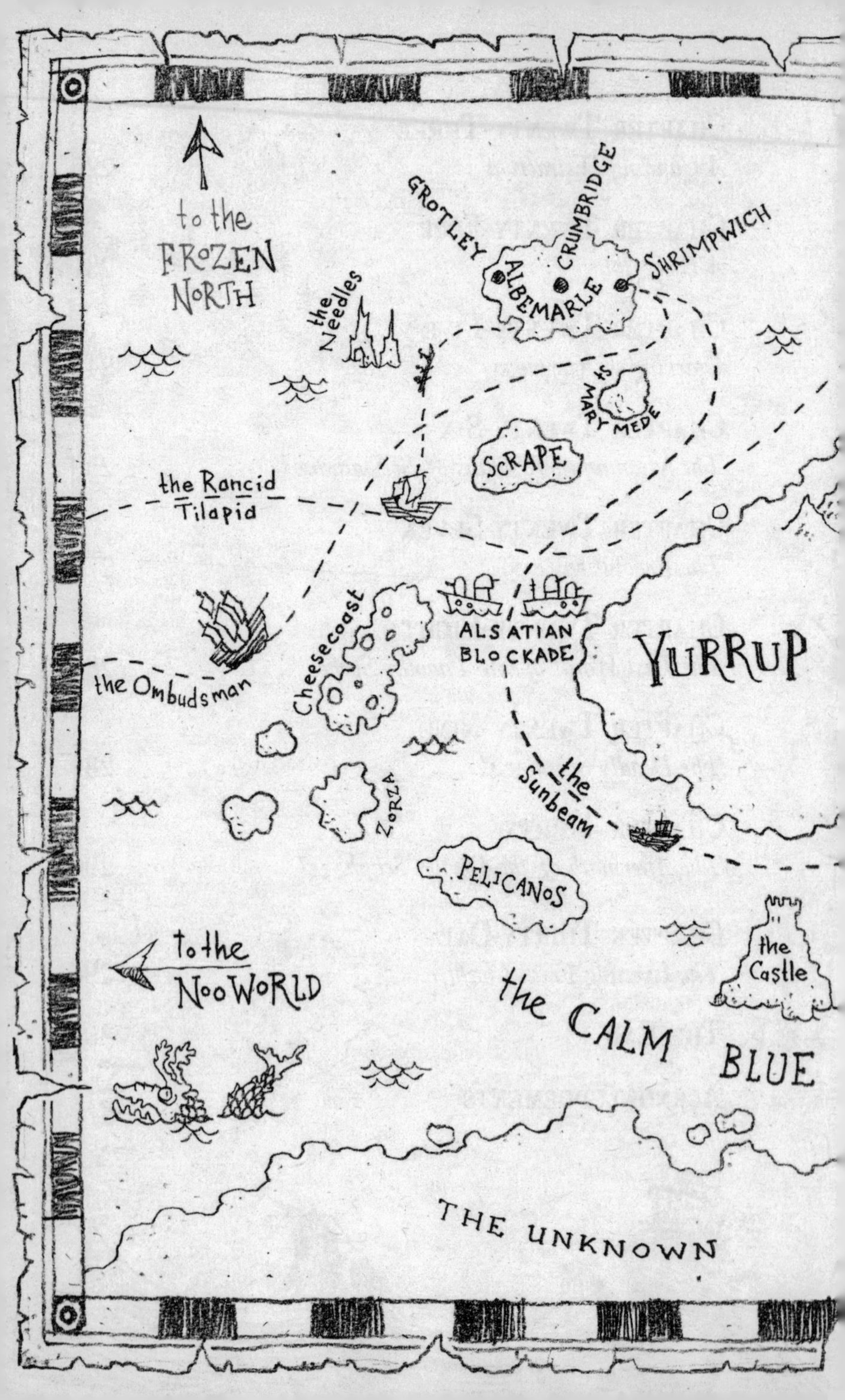

to the
FROZEN
NORTH
GROTLEY
CRUMBRIDGE
SHRIMPWICH
ALBEMARLE
the Needles
St MARY MEDE
SCRAPE
the Rancid
Tilapia
ALSATIAN
BLOCKADE
YURRUP
Cheesecoast
the Ombudsman
the
Sunbeam
ZORZA
PELICANOS
the
Castle
to the
NOOWORLD
the CALM
BLUE
THE UNKNOWN

SNOOD
BLACK FOREST
ALSATIA
OTOM
NEVER-ENDING WASTELANDS
the NEAR FAR EAST
DUSTY RED MOUNTAINS
SEA
ZINDERNEUF

THE END

Not long after you've finished reading this sentence, the whole hooman race will become extinct.

I say the *whole* hooman race, but that's not exactly true. Some of them will survive, but only a few. A pawful at most.

It's one of these survivors in whom we are *particularly* interested. Her name, as you have probably guessed from the front cover of this book, is Mabel Jones.

Poor young nose-picking Mabel Jones. Mabel Jones, who skipped the fate the rest of you will suffer, by virtue of being **snatched** from the present and pulled deep into the footure: a footure without hoomans.

How this happened is not important, but the end result *is*. Because, if Mabel Jones can work out what caused the end of the hooman race, maybe – just maybe – she can stop it happening . . .

Take a second.

Take a deep breath.

Take a biscuit from the biscuit tin and ponder this *unlikeliest* of heroes.

A mere child. All thin legs and scrawny shoulders. Scrawny shoulders that carry the greatest of weights.

The fate of the HOOMAN RACE!

CHAPTER ONE
A Relic from a Hooman Age

This is the life, eh?

You, me and a tiny rowing boat dwarfed by the gargantuan waves of the **WILD WESTERN SEA**! Sure, the salty wind **lashes** against my cheeks like an angry bosun's whip, but that's what happens if you gamble and lose your trousers in a game of cards at the CADAVEROUS LOBSTER TAVERN.

Still, there is something magical about the **WILD WESTERN SEA**, thinks I, as I lie back, gaze lazily at the stars and feel the cooling breeze around my –

I didn't say you could stop rowing!

We are drawing nearer to our goal. See there! Two dull shapes on the horizon. One large – a merchantman sailing from **ALBEMARLE**, I'll warrant. Probably the **OMBUDSMAN**, bound for the **NOO WORLD**. The other one is smaller, faster and closing in.

Is this it?

Is this the ship we seek?

Aye! I think it must be, for a flag is hoisted, and on that flag is a picture of a white ant on a background of inky blue-black. This is the RANCID TILAPIA, a pirate ship, captained by CAPTAIN RUFUS SICKLESMEAR THE YOUNGER.

Sicklesmear is a pirate of the old school – an aardvark with a wooden leg, a wooden nose and a habit of performing the foulest of acts, including kidnap, blackmail and throwing his dung at a security guard during a public reading of his autobiography, A NOSE FOR PIRACY. But it is not him we *really* seek. It is a member of his crew. A hooman. Our hero, Mabel Jones.

DID YOU HEAR THAT?!

The distant sound of cannon fire!

Row faster, reader, for we are missing the action. A sea battle is under way! Row! Row **faster**, lest we miss the gratuitous bloodshed. For our story is about to begin . . .

A Relic from a Hooman Age

In the hold of the RANCID TILAPIA, Mabel Jones's scrawny shoulders lie hunched beneath dribble-stained blankets, swinging in a hammock with every pitch and roll. She groans and tosses in her sleep. Her tattered and torn pyjamas are sodden with sweat.

Mabel Jones is deep within a dream.

A *bad* dream.

Can you pass me the Weetabix, Dad?

Dad?

DAD?

Her father breaks a sad, single segment from a satsuma and hands it to Mabel's baby sister, Maggie.

Mum, what's up with Dad?

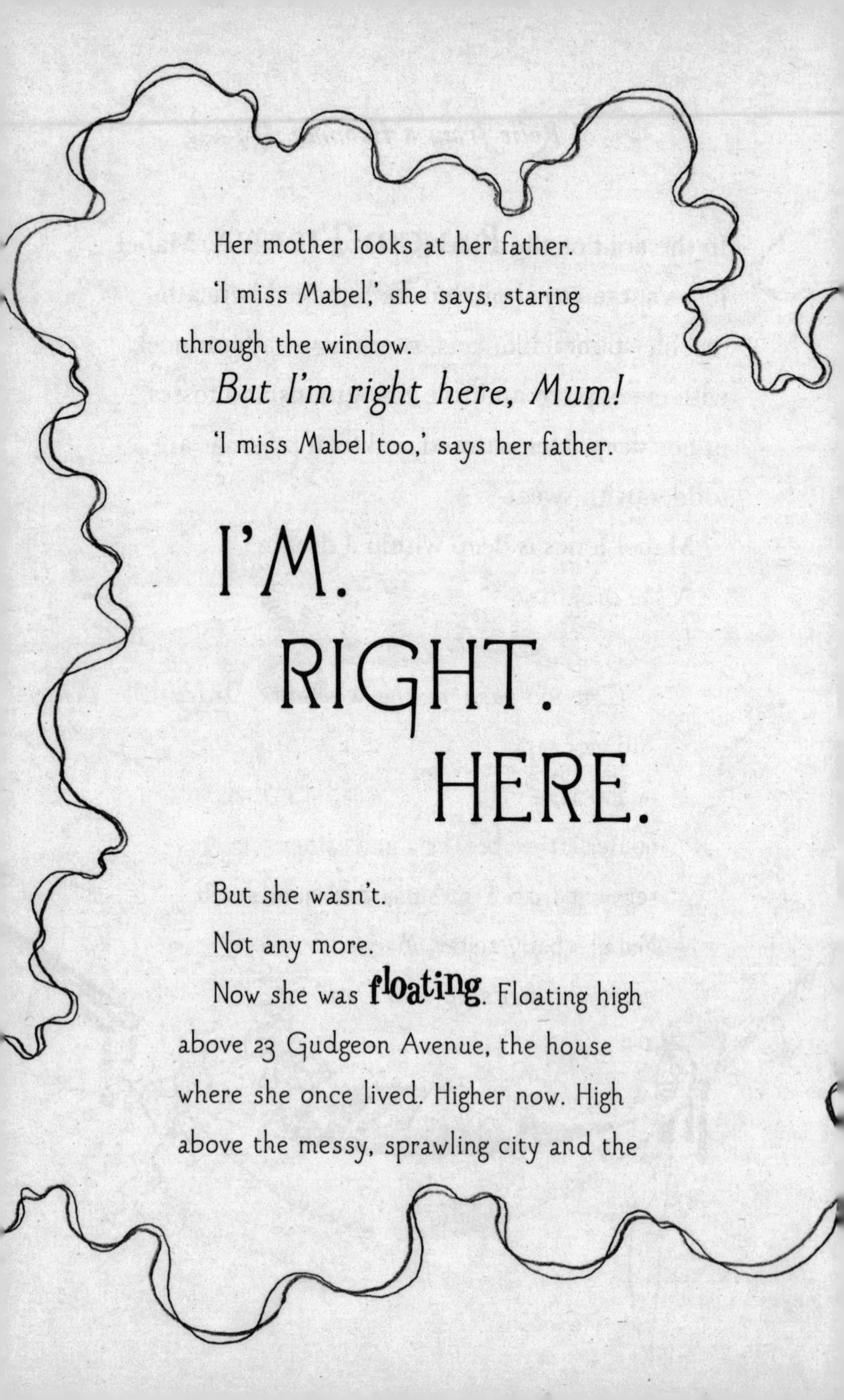

Her mother looks at her father.

'I miss Mabel,' she says, staring through the window.

But I'm right here, Mum!

'I miss Mabel too,' says her father.

I'M.

RIGHT.

HERE.

But she wasn't.

Not any more.

Now she was **floating**. Floating high above 23 Gudgeon Avenue, the house where she once lived. Higher now. High above the messy, sprawling city and the

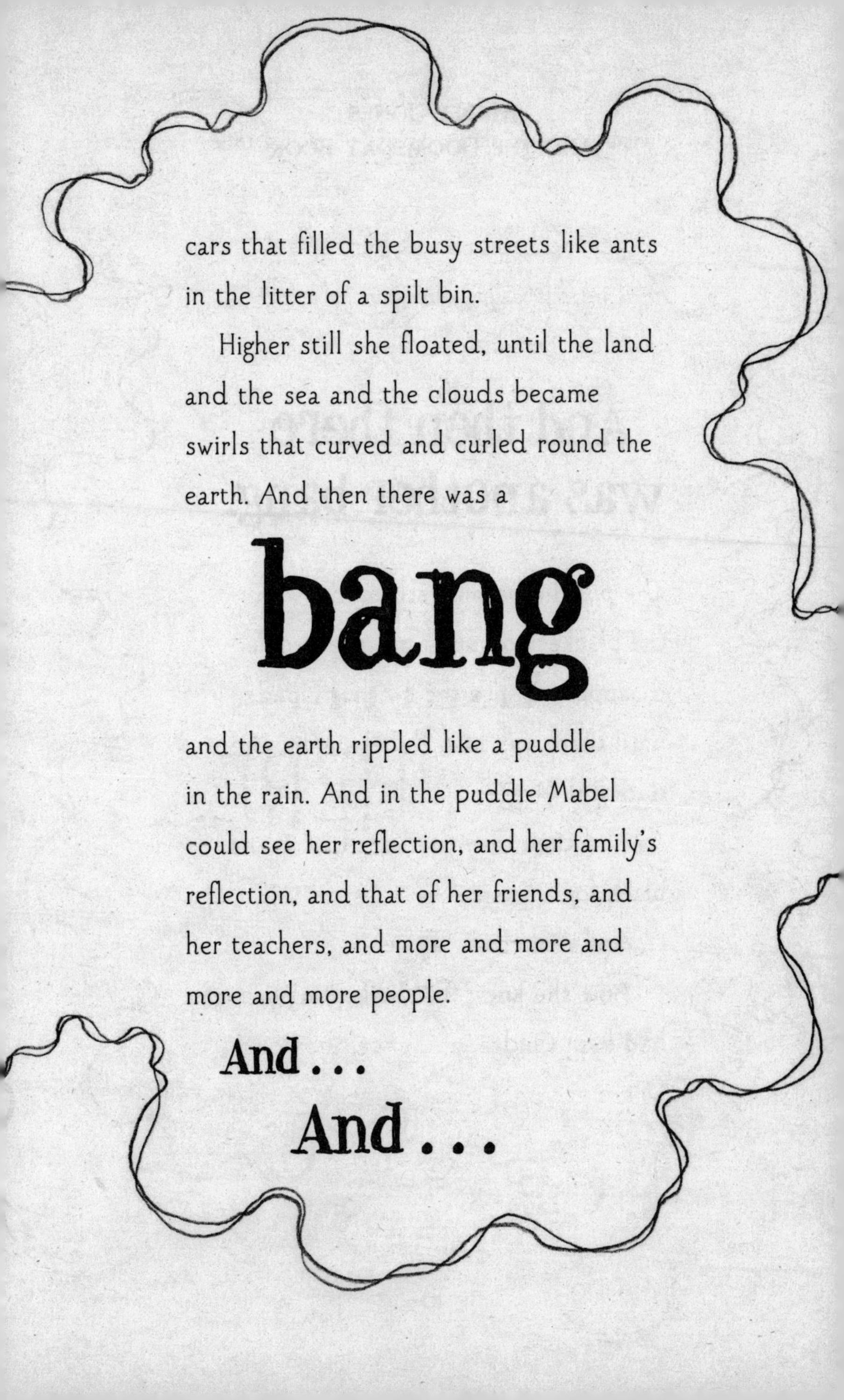

cars that filled the busy streets like ants in the litter of a spilt bin.

Higher still she floated, until the land and the sea and the clouds became swirls that curved and curled round the earth. And then there was a

bang

and the earth rippled like a puddle in the rain. And in the puddle Mabel could see her reflection, and her family's reflection, and that of her friends, and her teachers, and more and more and more and more people.

And . . .

And . . .

And then there was another bang.

The puddle became stir-murky with the blackest of mud, and the people disappeared into the swirling clouds, until there was just Mabel's mum and dad and Maggie.

And then they too were lost in the black fog.

And Mabel was alone.

And she knew that something bad had happened.

Mabel Jones sat up and rubbed the memories of the bad dream from her eyes. The whale-fat lamp swung with the pitch and roll of the RANCID TILAPIA and illuminated the snoring form of her crewmate 'Greasy' Daniel Lanolin-Flannel, an old sheep sleeping off the effects of last night's rum.

Voices were shouting from above:

'All hands on deck! Prepare to attack!'

Mabel sighed. Being a pirate was hard work.

Dangerous work.

She reached for the cutlass that hung from her hammock and prepared herself for another bloody sea battle.

MABEL JONES
AND THE DOOMSDAY BOOK

'My name is Mabel Jones
and I'm not scared
of anything.'

CHAPTER TWO

Another Bloody Sea Battle

Squat safely behind this crate of highly explosive gunpowder. Keep your head low and your tail, if you have one, tucked in. I cannot guarantee your safety, for a **bloody sea battle** carries a degree of risk for even the most cautious of observers, and more still for its active participants. In fact, we can identify any number of potential fates that might befall attacking pirates as they board an enemy ship.

Pass the popcorn.

FATE 1: Young Eriks

See Young Eriks high up the rigging of the RANCID TILAPIA? He's a keen young rodent and cabin hamster to Captain Sicklesmear. Cutlass in one hand, he grabs a thick, hairy rope with the other and swings! Curse those caterpillars of the infamous **vine moth**, and curse their hunger for thick, hairy ropes. The cord snaps and Young Eriks is plunged forever deep into the cold waters of the **WILD WESTERN SEA**, never to be seen again.

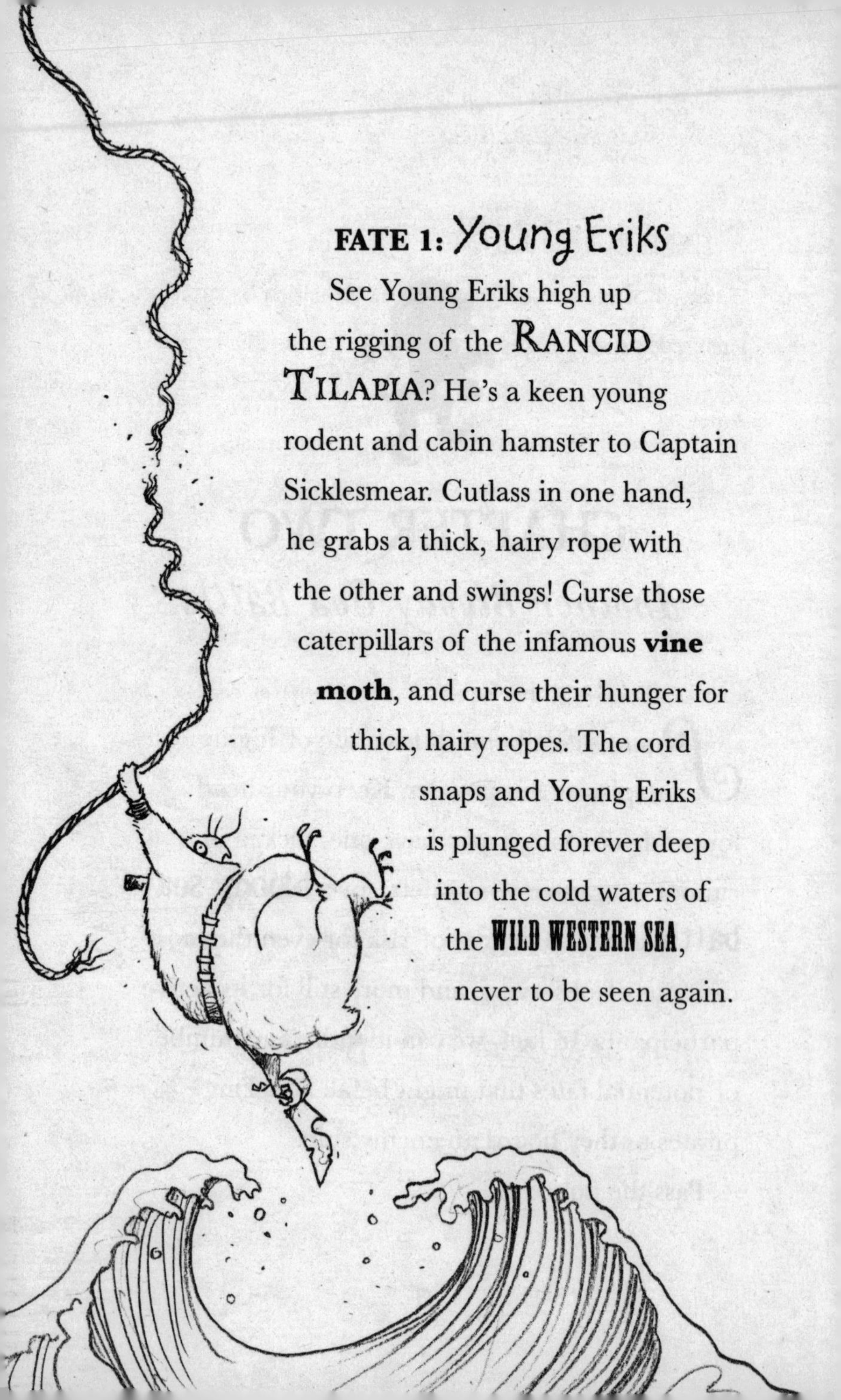

FATE 2: OTUS SLUGGARD

Otus Sluggard, a rare wet-nosed sloth, is next on this grisly list. This is supposed to be his last-ever voyage aboard the RANCID TILAPIA, for on a far-off clifftop overlooking a distant sea his fiancée Doreen awaits, a flower anxiously clasped between her three toes as she watches the horizon for a sign of his return.

Sadly, with but a single foot aboard the **OMBUDSMAN**, his innards meet with a well-aimed musket ball, and Doreen is doomed to wait forever.

FATE 3: CAPTAIN PEBBLEDASH of the **OMBUDSMAN**

The **OMBUDSMAN** has been overrun by pirates from the RANCID TILAPIA, and the smell of spent gunpowder is thick in the air. The two crews are locked in **deadly** paw-to-paw combat. The sounds of clashing cutlasses, pained screams and whimpered surrenders spoil the salty breeze. Through the terror, the smoke and the smell of musket fire, a figure emerges.

Mabel Jones!

Cutlass in her hand, she parries a blow from a passing tapir and leaps up to the helm where a Dalmatian stands. He is Captain Pebbledash of the **OMBUDSMAN**, and this is his first crossing of the **WILD WESTERN SEA**. He fires his flintlock pistol, but too early, and it discharges through his holster and into his foot. Before he realizes what has happened, a cutlass is pointed at his heart. The battle is over. The **OMBUDSMAN** has fallen to the pirates of the **RANCID TILAPIA** and Mabel Jones is victori–

FATE 4: Mabel Jones

Back in the hold of the RANCID TILAPIA, the sheep Greasy Daniel Lanolin-Flannel, still drunk from the night before, lights his pipe, rolls from his hammock, trips, falls on a cannon (match still aflame) and accidentally triggers the weapon. A heavy iron **cannonball** shoots through the side of the **OMBUDSMAN**, deflects off a reinforced barrel of sardines and smashes a massive hole in the deck. A hole through which Mabel Jones is now **fal**

CHAPTER THREE

It's Easy Being a Pirate

Mabel Jones winced.

She was lying on her back in the darkened hold of the **OMBUDSMAN**. A table had broken her fall, and her fall had broken a table.

Slowly her eyes became accustomed to the gloom. She was in a small private cabin. By the flickering light of a whale-fat lamp Mabel could see a large wooden chest had been upturned by her sudden arrival, its contents spilt across the floor.

Gold coins!

Thousands of them.

Above, the sound of fighting continued. Mabel carefully tucked her trusty cutlass into her belt and picked her nose thoughtfully.

What could I do with all this gold?

A new cutlass?

A new ship?

My own ship?

A scrap of paper among the gold caught her eye. A page carefully torn from a notebook not unlike the one she had once used at school.

She picked it up. The paper was yellowed and a bit crumbly.

It must be ancient!

It had a sentence written on it in spidery handwriting, but in the flickering gloom Mabel could only make out one word:

Doomsday

'Once I get back into the light I'll be able to read it all,' she said to herself.

Mabel picked her nose and looked around at the gold coins strewn about the wrecked cabin.

It was easy being a pirate.

Maybe too easy . . .

Something was wrong!

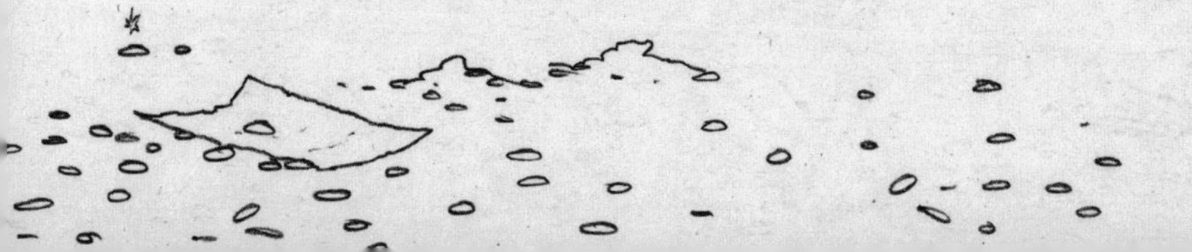

Her hand grasped the hilt of her cutlass.

'Stop right there!' said a voice.

Mabel turned to face the speaker.

Sitting in a comfortable-looking leather armchair was a smartly dressed warthog. In one trotter he held a glass of port; in the other, a pistol.

The pistol was pointed at her heart.

'For a pirate, you seem awfully interested in a scrap of paper, eh?'

The warthog smiled. Beneath his side-whiskers and moustachioed snout, Mabel could see a threatening pair of tusks.

'Why don't you put it down here, on the arm of my chair? Slowly, though, eh? I don't want to make any more mess.'

Mabel carefully placed the note down.

'Pirates!' the warthog snorted. 'The **lowest** form of crook. Worse pay than a pickpocket in a poorhouse. No, there's no profit in piracy.'

He took a sip of port. 'I could teach you a thing or two about stealing, eh? I, SIR LEOPOLD GUPPY, have stolen more money than your puny brain could ever imagine, eh? And how? I'm a corrupt banker – that's how!'

He laughed again.

'Stealing from the poor is the most fun. Their pitiful life savings might be mere piffle to a hog of my financial status, but their suffering is **enjoyable** to me.'

'You're disgusting!' snarled Mabel Jones, her grip tightening on the hilt of her cutlass. 'You think money is more important than being kind!'

Guppy smiled and downed the last of his port.

'Oh, it's not just money. I also take things of purely sentimental value.' He nodded towards the arm of his chair. 'That is a piece of **holy paper**, would you believe! Supposedly from an ancient book!'

'Where did you get it?' asked Mabel.

The warthog smirked.

'From a convent on the coast of **ALBEMARLE** – part payment for a debt. The Mother Superior says it's a relic from the hooman age. It's the only thing of value she had. She really didn't want to part with it, eh? But I insisted.'

Mabel Jones gasped.

'A relic from the hooman age'!

A minuscule spore of ***inspiration*** drifted into her head and settled gently on the mossy floor of her imagination.

This might be the clue I need to find out what happened to the human race!

'Give it to me,' said Mabel Jones. 'Please. I need it.'

Sir Leopold Guppy laughed cruelly.

'Oh you do, do you? I suppose I could let you have it. It means nothing to me really. Just a tiny scrap of wealth compared to the vast fortune here!'

Then his smiling, gloating face turned to an angry frown.

'But if you think you can drop in here through a hole in the ceiling and steal from me you're sorely mistaken. Because it's *mine*. ALL OF IT.

EVERY.

LAST.

PENNY.

EH?'

He took a deep breath and wiped frothing spittle from his whiskers with a silken hankie.

'So I can do whatever I want with it.'

And, with that, Guppy held the paper out towards the flame of the whale-fat lamp.

'No!

Don't!'

cried Mabel Jones.

But she was too late. She could only watch as the flame turned the ancient paper to **ash**.

'And as for you, girl, I'm afraid you'll have to pay a hefty fee for trying to rob me of my ill-gotten gains.'

Sir Leopold Guppy's trotter tightened on the trigger.

'I'm closing your account!'

There is *a moment* before you die.

A **stretched** **second** that contains the memories of a life about to end.

Mum.

Dad.

Maggie!

Mabel missed them so much, and in that **stretched** **second** she felt further from her own home and further from her own time than she had ever felt before.

Mabel Jones closed her eyes and waited to die . . .

Everything was silent.

Suspiciously silent.

Mabel Jones opened a single eye, just a little bit.

Then she opened it all the way.

Then she opened the other eye.

Sir Leopold Guppy had been bagged in a suspiciously banker-shaped sack. Next to the sack stood Mabel's friend, one Omynus Hussh, a silent loris. The silent loris, should you not be aware of such a creature, is a curious species – quiet and faithful like a shadow, sneaky as the **SKID MARKS** in an assassin's underpants.

He smiled at Mabel shyly, smoothing a bit of fur that grew in the wrong direction with a licked paw.

'Even without the proper fingers on my proper paws, I ties the knot that keeps the greedy wriggling-pigling safe inside.'

He proudly held up his left arm. Where a nimble-fingered paw should have been, a

doorknob was attached, a memento from the day he first met Mabel Jones (as detailed in the amazingly exciting book *The Unlikely Adventures of Mabel Jones* – available in all good bookshops*).

---

* And in bad ones too. Like the one in which you bought this book (one of the booksellers has pressed a bogey on page 134).

There was a **loud bang** and a splintering noise, and a goat's head appeared through a hole in the door. The goat smiled at Mabel. His crooked, pipe-smoke-stained teeth shone yellow in the lamplight.

'PELF!' said Mabel with a grin.

She may have been far from home, but it was good to have friends around, and this goat was a friend indeed. They had met on Mabel's first day in the footure, not long after she'd first been stolen from her own time to begin her most unlikely adventure. They'd shared many adventures since then, and if there was one thing that could be relied upon it was Pelf's loyalty to his friend Mabel. Well, that and his famously **bad breath**.

'The battle be won and the loot is to be shared among our fellow pirates . . .'

His voice trailed off as he saw the chest of golden coins.

'Aha! Booty! And lots of it!'

The suspiciously banker-shaped sack wriggled angrily.

'You'll pay for this, you miserable nobodies!' exclaimed a muffled voice. 'I'll hunt you down. Nobody messes with Sir Leopold Guppy.'

Pelf looked at Mabel.

'Who?'

Mabel shrugged. 'It doesn't matter.'

Pelf removed his head from the hole, and the door swung open. A hooman boy, a little smaller and a little younger than Mabel, stood beside the goat pirate. His face was smudged with the **grime of battle**.

'Hi, **JARVIS**,' said Mabel.

What do we know about Jarvis? His time in the footure is well documented – a sidekick to Mabel Jones on her previous unlikely adventures – but we know little of his life in the past. Perhaps all will be revealed later in the story.*

Jarvis blinked.

'We need to get this money back to the RANCID TILAPIA. The look-out's spotted the **ALBEMARLE NAVY** on the horizon.'

Pelf sucked on his pipe and blew out a cloud of thoughtful smoke, which gathered wisely around his head.

'Aye, it does no good hanging around the scene of a crime! If the Albemarle Navy are nearby,

---

* Or perhaps not. I haven't decided yet.

we're further east than I thought.' He tugged his beard worriedly. 'There be a hefty punishment for piracy in their waters. Besides, we'll be needing to share the booty out, as according to pirate law!'

Mabel pursed her lips. The minuscule spore of *inspiration* that had drifted on to the mossy floor of her imagination some moments earlier had suddenly mushroomed into a fully formed fungus of a plan.

She smiled at her pirate friends. It was the kind of smile you smile when you've just had the kind of thought that starts a new unlikely adventure.

'Actually I've got a **better** idea, and I think you're going to like it!'

CHAPTER FOUR
A Bad Idea

'I don't like this idea. I don't like it at all,' grumbled Pelf as he leapt from the lifeboat of the **OMBUDSMAN** and began to drag it up through the shallows and on to the sandy beach of a small cove. The moon was full and lit the **JAGGED BLACK CLIFFS** that surrounded them on all sides.

He sucked on his pipe and looked around nervously. 'It goes against nature, it does. Against nature *and* against pirate law!'

Mabel jumped overboard to help her friend.

'But don't you see, Pelf? If the Mother Superior has a book from the hooman age, she might know how the hooman race went extinct!'

Pelf shrugged.

'But, snuglet, Captain Sicklesmear will be angrier than an orca in a duck pond! What happened in the past be of no interest to us pirates. It's **gold** that be interesting!'

Mabel frowned. 'This money was stolen from the poor. We should give it back to the poor.'

Jarvis unrolled a map stolen from the **OMBUDSMAN**. 'Here it is: ST HILDA'S CONVENT AND HOME FOR THE ORPHANED YOUNG OF THE GROTLEY TIN MINES. They'll be glad of the money!'

Pelf shook his head mournfully. 'The fourth of the seven pirate sins: **charity**! The only graver sin is **bathing**!'

For those of you unfamiliar with the seven

pirate sins (usually handed down from pirate to pirate in hushed and fearful voices), they appear written **for the first time ever** below.

THE SEVEN DEADLY PIRATE SINS

1. *Snitching*
2. *Mercy*
3. *Bathing*
4. *Charity*
5. *Cake-baking*
7. *Maths*

Pelf looked up at the craggy black cliffs and shuddered.

'Dry land! I hate it. I'll have no part of this. I'll be waiting for ye here, once yer foul deed be complete. I've a pouch full of **Bumbeard & Sons** tobacco that I've been looking forward to popping into my pipe.'

Omynus Hussh looked at Mabel with his big brown eyes.

'Can I comes, Mabel?'

'Of course you can,' said Mabel Jones, smiling and scratching the top of his head. Then she stopped and peered at him through squinty eyes. 'As long as you don't **steal** anything. We're giving the treasure back, remember?'

Omynus blinked.

'I promises. I is doing my bestest to stop my stealings.' He puffed out his little chest. 'Even if I is the bestest thief ever!'

Pelf sat in the lifeboat and watched as Jarvis,

Mabel and Omynus lugged the chest of doubloons towards a steep and winding path that led up the cliff face. He shook his head sadly.

'Mark my words: no good will come of this. No good at all . . .'

Hold tightly to that rusting weathervane, for this storm shows no sign of stopping! The convent to the roof of which you currently cling has stood for hundreds of years against the **ravages** of the wet winds that sweep across the desolate moor.

But times are hard in this part of **ALBEMARLE**, especially for poor nuns. The tiles flap in the breeze and the guttering hangs loose from its fixings.

Why are we here, you ask, clinging on for dear life?

The answer lies in the darkness, wandering towards us across the moor: a tiny light in the gloom. A whale-fat lamp stolen from the cabin of Sir Leopold Guppy illuminates the most silent of creatures as he picks his way through a **treacherous mire**, cautiously testing the firmness of the ground with each step.

It is Omynus Hussh!

Behind him the two snuglets, Mabel and Jarvis, struggle with a chest. A casket full of doubloons is a heavy load, and one wrong step in the darkness could send both of them down to a

slow

and

terrible

death,

sucked deep beneath the surface of the bog. Slowly, step by step, they reach the firmer ground at the foot of the crumbling stone walls of ST HILDA'S CONVENT AND HOME FOR THE ORPHANED YOUNG OF THE GROTLEY TIN MINES. A bell rope is pulled and a small figure welcomes them in from the storm.

Quickly, slide down the roof. It's been a week since the last lightning strike upon this spire, and I wouldn't want to bet against it happening again tonight. See that drainpipe? The one with the rusting brackets that pull away from the crumbling wall? Climb down it.

Halfway to the ground is the fourth floor. If you stretch across to that ledge, it will give you access to the broken window. Put your arm through the jagged hole and open it from the inside. Now carefully climb inside the room. And you're here! In the office of the Mother Superior, MOTHER AGNES, an ageing duck with eyes as bright as her feathers are dulled.

Me?

Where am I?

Oh, I'm here already. I took the stairs.

Silence your whining words! For there are footsteps outside, and the door is beginning to open . . .

Mother Agnes peered over the top of her spectacles at the open casket of gold that sat on her desk.

'Well,' she said, 'in all my time as MOTHER SUPERIOR I have never received a donation as generous as yours.'

Mabel jigged in excitement.

'There's **loads** in there. You can have it all!'

The old duck smiled. It was a kind of favourite-teacher smile, crinkly round the eyes and beak, which made Mabel feel all warm inside.

Mother Agnes looked at Mabel. Then she looked at Jarvis. Then she looked at Omynus Hussh, who was hiding behind Mabel's legs.

'But will one of you *please* explain how you came to be in possession of such enormous wealth?'

Mabel shuffled her feet guiltily and looked at

the floor in silence.

The nun turned to Jarvis, who was **coincidentally** looking out of the window.

Finally she turned to Omynus.

'Well?'

Mabel felt a cold, sweaty paw slide into her hand.

Mother Agnes frowned.

'Is this gold yours to give?'

Omynus rubbed the back of his head with his doorknobbed stump.

There was a long pause.

Then . . .

'We stoles it!' he blurted. 'We stoles it!'

Mother Agnes pursed her beak disapprovingly.

'Stolen gold! Well I never!'

Jarvis stepped forward.

'Twice-stolen, technically. Once from a **crooked banker**, then again from a **pirate captain**. There was a lot of fighting involved the first time; the second time was more **sneaky** . . .'

His voice trailed off as he noticed Mother Agnes's steely glare.

'It was Mabel's idea,' he added.

Mother Agnes pursed her beak even more.

'We took it from Sir Leopold Guppy,' explained Mabel. 'He stole it from the poor and needy, so we thought we ought to give it back.'

Mother Agnes unpursed her beak.

'Sir Leopold Guppy, you say? That horrible hog! He's been squeezing money out of the convent for years. Well, even if your means were naughty, I can see that your motives were true. And your donation could, no doubt, help the poor orphans of the Grotley Tin Mines. It could even pay to fix the convent roof. We might even be able to afford some new novices . . .'

She looked sadly over at a pile of empty habits and wimples in the corner.

'It seems no one wants to be a nun these days. No one apart from **Sister Miriam**, that is. She arrived just last week and is tending to the orphans as we speak.'

Mother Agnes sighed, removed her glasses and looked Mabel in the eye.

'Thank you for your donation, child. I'm delighted to accept it.'

'There was *one* other thing,' said Mabel as Mother Agnes locked the gold in a safe. 'Guppy also had an old piece of paper. From an ancient book or something. It got burnt in the battle, but he said he'd taken it from you.'

Mother Agnes sighed.

'Yes, he did. And may **ST STATHAM** forgive me for handing over something so sacred to that foul banker. It was the last remaining piece of an ancient book. That page had been held in the convent for hundreds of years. Alas, I had no choice but to give it to Guppy to pay our debts.

Stale bread doesn't come cheaply, you know.'

Mabel nodded sympathetically. 'He said it was from the hooman age. Is that true?'

Mother Agnes waddled to the window, hopped on to the window ledge and stared out across the rainswept moor.

'Yes. It was from an ancient book about the extinction of the hooman species. The book was entrusted to this convent many hundreds of years ago by a wandering missionary who'd found it in his tour of *The Unknown*. The name of that book was –'

Lightning flashed across the sky, followed swiftly by a roll of thunder.

'The name of that book was

THE

DOOMSDAY

BOOK!'

'So, if we can find that book, then it will tell us what happened to the hooman race!' exclaimed Jarvis excitedly.

Mother Agnes nodded sadly.

'Yes – but, alas, the book is not here. It was not kept at the convent for long. A year after it arrived, an outbreak of **beak droop** swept these parts and many of the nuns had to leave. The book was taken from here for safekeeping by the convent librarian. Only a single page was kept as a relic, until that horrid warthog took it.'

She took a **deep** **breath**.

'Forgive me, I am forgetting my manners. I guess you three little ones must be needing refreshment. I'm afraid we've not much to offer, but we will find something.'

Mother Agnes pulled on a bell rope suspended from the ceiling and a rabbit nun shuffled into the room. She glanced at Mabel with strangely bulging eyes.

'This is Sister Miriam. Sister, would you be a dear and warm some rum for the children? There may be some gruel left from the orphans' supper too.'

Sister Miriam nodded. 'Of course, Mother Agnes.'

The rabbit shuffled from the room, pausing to look at Mabel, Jarvis and Omynus once more, before slowly closing the door.

Mother Agnes smiled.

'In the meantime let me show you around. We do some tremendous work here with the orphans of the GROTLEY TIN MINES. I'm sure –'

A **loud ringing** interrupted her sentence.

Then banging.

Mother Agnes clasped her wings together anxiously. '*Two* sets of visitors in one night. Whatever next?'

There was more banging, then the sound of angry voices and an **even louder**

Splintering

sound. You'll be familiar with the particular type of splintering sound, I'm sure. It was *exactly* the kind of sound a heavy studded oak door makes when it is broken down by a squad of musket-wielding soldiers.

Now the sound of angry voices was joined by the sound of howling winds.

'Search the building!' a voice commanded.

'Three smugglers are in here somewhere and I want to see them hanging from the gibbet by dawn!'

It was A RAID!

CHAPTER FIVE
The Mystery of the Three Nuns

You have, of course, heard of the might of the **ALBEMARLE REDCOATS**, the greatest army in history. You will, I'm sure, have studied their **immense** global influence in your military warfare classes at school.

No?

Your teacher must be slacking. Too busy filling their face with digestive biscuits in the staffroom, I'll warrant. Maybe, just maybe, with their

last ounce of willpower they have prised themself away from the biscuit tin and are actually reading this to you now. Unlikely, I admit, but, if they are, take the opportunity to look at them with your most cherubic, innocent face and say:

Please, miss/Please, sir. We long to learn, and you are the one to help form us into worthy and knowledgeful hoomans. Please, we implore you, from the bottom of our pure and childlike hearts, to give up those biscuits and return to teaching.

And then add:

All your biscuits can be sent to the address at the back of this book, whereupon they will be ~~eaten~~ safely destroyed by the narrator.

Anyway, allow me to fill the **gap** in your woefully malformed education. It seems like a good time to unfold a mini-map of the **KNOWN WORLD**. It's in my pocket

somewhere . . .

Not those. I'm sure I put it in here this morning . . .

Or these. I know it's here somewhere . . .

For heaven's sake, it must be in here . . .

Aha! Here it is!

Allow me to unfold it across the next two pages.

MAP of the KNOWN WORLD

ALBEMARLE
ST MARY MEDE
SCRAPE
Cheesecoast
YURRU
ZORZA
PELICANOS
"the Castle"
to the NOO WORLD
the CALM BLUE
THE UNKNOWN
NEUTRAL TERRITORIES
ALSATIAN EMPIRE
ALBEMARLIAN EMPIRE

ALBEMARLE
GROTLEY
CRUMBRIDGE
SHRIMPWICH
TIN MINES
the Moors
St Hilda's
Secret Cove
the PROSPEROUS SOUTH
ALSATIAN SEA
OTOM
ZINDERNEUF
N
W
E
S

War is on the horizon.

And not just any war but a war between the two great superpowers of the footure. A war that started over a curious and unclaimed smell.

Whether it was **LADY MILLICENT POLECAT**, wife of the ambassador of **ALBEMARLE**, who released the scent, or her opposite at the dinner table that fateful night, the **Crown Princess Helga of Alsatia**, we will never know – for both ladies, globally admired for their refined beauty and stately graces, denied the expulsion of foul-smelling gas.

An official transcript of their discussion is available below.

Lady Millicent: There appears to be a strange smell originating from the Alsatian side of the table.

Princess Helga: To be correct, it appears to be wafting on the breeze from the side upon which the good lady of Albemarle sits.

Lady Millicent: I am sure an aroma of such perturbing distinction could only be the work of a foreign bottom.

Princess Helga: Is the good lady aware of the phrase 'Whosoever smelt it, dealt it'?

Further accusations were made.

Voices were **raised**.

And one hundred years of peaceful diplomacy were undone, all due to a

Now the two great empires of **ALBEMARLE** and **Alsatia** stood at the brink of war.

The **ALBEMARLE EMPIRE** was once respected across the seven seas for its culture, imposed far and wide by its particularly ruthless and well-trained army, nicknamed Redcoats after their brightly coloured jackets. Alas for **ALBEMARLE**, its position in today's world is uncertain. Technological advancements have led to the rise of other powers and **ALBEMARLE** seems stuck in the past. For example, their red coats, once the pride of the brave soldiers who wore them, are now more widely praised by their enemies, who use them to spot **ALBEMARLE** soldiers from far away and pick them off with the latest model of long-range muskets.

But still they have their heroes. Take **CAPTAIN HEATHCLIFFE STREEP**, for example. A particularly handsome pedigree Labrador, with tours of duty in the **NOO WORLD** and the Dusty Red Mountains that lie west of the Near Far East. Streep is skilled in musketry, horsemanship, sabre-wielding and shouting motivational slogans over the sound of overwhelming enemy cannon fire. **Taut muscles** strain against his tight red military-issue jacket, and his face radiates good looks and the finest of **inbreeding**. You can bask in his glory now, for here he is, striding heroically into the room to arrest our three heroes for smuggling.

BUT WAIT! What trickery is this? Where *are* Mabel, Omynus and Jarvis?

They have disappeared!

Captain Heathcliffe Streep, the particularly handsome Labrador, looked along the length of his sabre and was relieved to see it was, as always, looking **exceedingly** sharp and shiny.

Then he paced the room, pausing to look from the old stone window across the wet and windy moonlit moor. He shuddered and spun round in his polished boots to raise a suspicious eyebrow at Mother Agnes, Sister Miriam and the three other nuns that, **strangely**, we didn't notice earlier.

Where *did* those three extra nuns come from?

'You see, it's really most odd, Mother Agnes. Three sets of footprints lead from the not-so-secret cove straight to your convent, and yet when we arrive to apprehend these smugglers they have disappeared!'

He turned to his sergeant, a similarly attired (but dirtier) sheep.

'Any further developments, **GUBBINS**?'

'No, sir. We've circled the convent twice and no tracks lead out. They must *still* be here, sir!'

He eyed the three nuns suspiciously.

'Sir, do you think it's possible that the three smugglers have disguised themselves as –'

'Quiet, Gubbins! I'm thinking . . .'

Captain Streep rubbed his muzzle thoughtfully.

'Yes, Mother Agnes. Quite the riddle . . .'

He looked at the three nuns, who stood quietly behind Sister Miriam, heads bowed in quiet contemplation.

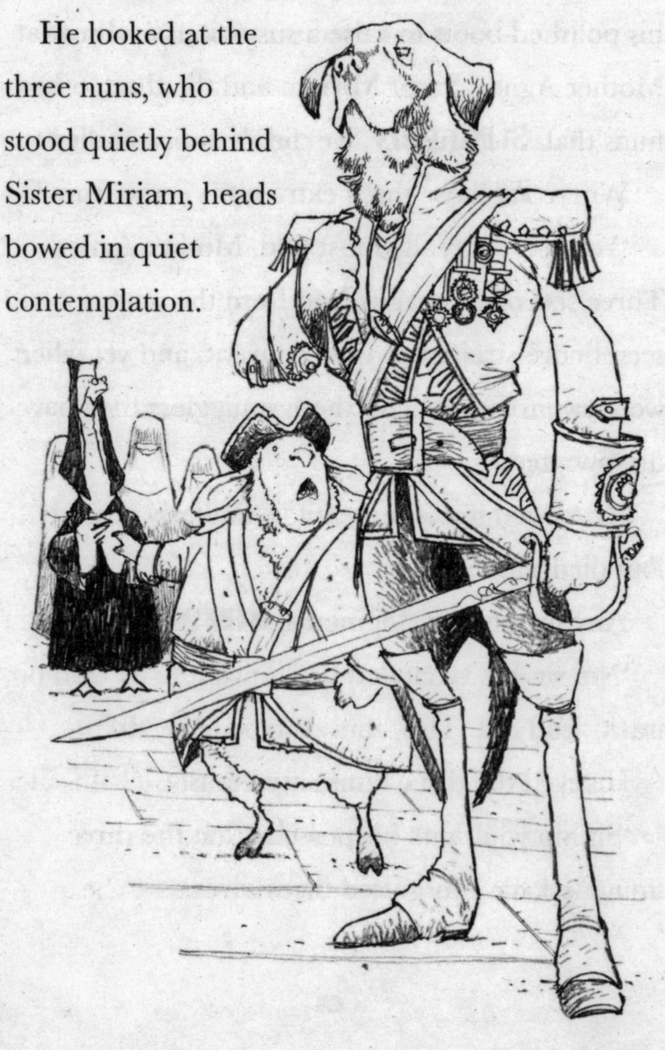

'I don't suppose you three saw anything? Any smugglers? They'd have muddy feet, a bit like those, I suppose.' He pointed at the feet of the tallest nun, who shuffled a muddy rabbit slipper back beneath her habit.

The three nuns shook their heads solemnly.

Mother Agnes smiled **politely** at the captain.

'I'm afraid these novices have sworn an oath of silence. Now, if you don't mind, captain, they must attend to the orphans. Sisters, if you will?'

Gubbins coughed pointedly as the nuns shuffled towards the door.

'Sir, do you think we should at least ask these three nuns to provide some form of identification?'

Streep turned to Gubbins and laughed.

'Paperwork, Gubbins? Really?' He shook his head. 'You've a lot to learn of the military life, Gubbins. One must always act on **instinct**! Instinct honed on the field of battle.' His eyes took on a far-away look. 'Those were the days. Oh, to be at war again. Better than patrolling these godforsaken moors looking for smugglers! Dash this place! The damp makes my fur completely unmanageable.'

He slashed his sabre at an imaginary foe, then paused suddenly to sigh.

'Oh well, they've escaped this time. I'm afraid we'll only be able to hang the goat we found asleep in the cove.'

The first and tallest of the three nuns paused in the doorway and began to turn, as if to say something. Then she stopped, as if the thing she had wanted to say would be better said later, or not at all.

'Here! I'll get that for you, ma'am,' said Captain Streep, holding the door and **bowing politely**.

'Thanks,' said the middle-sized nun sworn to a vow of silence in a distinctly boyish voice.

'My pleasure,' replied Streep. 'What is it *now*, Gubbins?'

Gubbins was tugging at his sleeve.

'Sir, sir, I really think we should –'

Captain Streep frowned at the sheep.

'Silence, Gubbins!

Any more of your impertinence and I'll have you before a court martial!'

And, with that, he spun on the heel of his finely polished boot and paced handsomely from the room.

CHAPTER SIX
The Creaking Gibbet

Welcome to **CRUMBRIDGE**, the capital city of **ALBEMARLE**! But, please, stop dawdling.

There is little time to amble along the gentle **RIVER CRUMB**, nor to pause to listen to the birdsong that drifts across the calm water, punctuated only by occasional bursts of **bad poetry** from the courting couples that sit on the river's grassy banks. There's less time still to explore the splendid town centre: a maze of charming **cobbled streets** and small squares. And no time at all to behold the historic **UNIVERSITY OF CRUMBRIDGE**, with its tall and crooked spire that rises high above the rooftops.

Luckily the students of Crumbridge are young and their minds are occupied with complex academic issues. This makes it easier to steal their bicycles.

Pedal fast, reader, while I perch in the basket. We need to get to the main square.

Take a look at this!

I found it pasted to a letter box.

A great injustice is to be committed!

Sponsored by Guppy & Sons Investment Bank
and Wilkins Picnic Accessories of Crumbridge

THE MAIN EVENT

Her Majesty's Hangman requests the pleasure of your company for

THE EXECUTION OF

PELF THE PIRATE GOAT

who will be hanged by the neck from the creaking gibbet until most definitely dead on the very serious charges of Smuggling Tobacco, Piracy, Foul Language, False Witness, Body Odour, Bad Teeth and a general lack of moral fibre.

* * *

Whereupon a cream tea will be served.
Then, for your further entertainment,

THE EXECUTION OF

STABBY JOE
AND
BLIND HAROLD

for the crimes of Robbery, Extortion and Nudism.

AND THE SPECIAL-EDITION
BONUS EXECUTION OF

THE PARK LANE POISONER

Crime: Garlic Dealing.

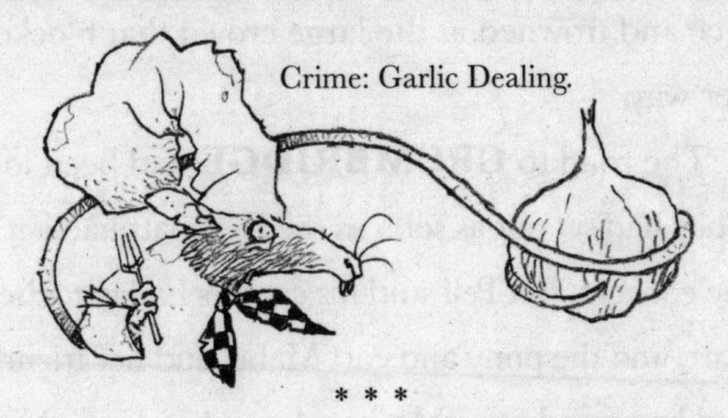

* * *

* NEW FEATURE *

THE PUBLIC APPLICATION OF 72 LASHES TO

BILLY SCRIBBINS

aka Sir Peregrine Wimpole aka THE FALSE TOFF for the serious crimes of Airs and Graces, Incorrect Schooling and the Tying of a Windsor Knot in an Improper Fashion.

ALSO FEATURING:

CUCUMBER SANDWICHES, TOMBOLA, CHARITY RAFFLE, CHILDREN'S ACTIVITY TENT and THE 27th ANNUAL DUCKING OF THE CRUMBRIDGE CRONE.

Mabel Jones picked some dried mud from her face and frowned at the large crowd that blocked her way.

The road to **CRUMBRIDGE** had been long. They had set out as soon as the Redcoats had left the convent, but Pelf and his captors had got a head start, and the pony and cart Mabel and her friends had borrowed from Mother Agnes had been slow – especially since the pony insisted on stopping every half an hour for a **manure break**.

First he had taken the friends north, along the only road that wound through the moors. Then they turned eastwards on the potholed highway that cut a brown scar through the gently rolling countryside. They slept whenever the **bumpy** road allowed, taking it in turns to steer the grumbling pony.

Now they were in Crumbridge, a beautiful city built on the banks of the gently winding **RIVER CRUMB**. But Mabel and her friends had no time to admire the cobbled streets or dreaming spires, for their important mission to discover what had happened to the hooman race had been postponed for something even more important . . .

TO RESCUE THEIR FRIEND PELF BEFORE HE WAS

H A N G E D

BY THE NECK UNTIL MOST DEFINITELY

DEAD!

Mabel, Jarvis and Omynus abandoned the pony and pushed through the crowded square. All around, badgers, weasels, moles and the like were picnicking, chattering and enjoying the fabulous sunshine that shone down on the grand and beautiful buildings of Crumbridge. The male creatures were all wearing **blazers** and **straw boaters**, while parasols and **polite blushing** were the order of the day for the ladies. A small wolf cub walked through the square, selling tubs of ice cream, mini Albemarle flags and souvenir execution bookmarks.

'Look!' cried Jarvis.

Rising from the middle of the square, surrounded by a double row of musket-wielding Redcoats, a wooden platform had been erected. On the wooden platform was a timber frame that creaked in the warm breeze. A single rope hung from a beam, and at the end of the rope was tied

. . . A NOOSE!

IT WAS THE CREAKING GIBBET!

And even worse . . .

Standing on a trapdoor on the platform . . .

Head poking through the noose . . .

A smokeless pipe hanging forlornly from his mouth . . .

Stood Pelf.

Mabel's heart skipped a beat.

Not Pelf.

Please, not my Pelf!

Omynus's large eyes blinked up at her. A salty tear rolled down his furry face.

'Can we saves him from the deadly dangling, Mabeljones?'

Jarvis put his arm round Omynus's shoulder.

'Mabel will think of something – won't you, Mabel?'

Mabel swallowed hard.

But what if I can't? What if I don't have a plan this time?

The executioner, a skunk, checked his watch.

A military drummer started a slow drum roll.

The crowd fell into a hushed silence.

And Mabel knew that it was too late.

She tried to push through the soldiers, but it was useless. There were too many. They stood five-deep round the platform.

'PELF!' she cried.

Suddenly Mabel felt a comforting paw on her shoulder and heard a voice in her ear.

'Calm yourself, Mabel Jones. There is another way to save your friend.'

Mabel spun round.

The speaker was an elderly dog dressed in a crumpled corduroy suit, leaning for support upon a battered silver-topped cane.

His eyes sparkled behind a pair of spectacles.

'How do you know my name?' demanded Mabel.

The old hound smiled and his eyes twinkled even more.

'It's my job to know things, Mabel.' He looked up at the gibbet. 'But what I want to know right now is what you would be willing to do to save your friend.'

'Anything!' replied Mabel.

'Anything?'

'**Anything!** Please!'

The dog smiled and handed Mabel a business card.

Then he turned and limped away into the crowd. As he went, he pulled a faded handkerchief from his corduroy suit and blew his nose.

High above the crowd, a **squirrel** watching the execution from a bedroom window saw the handkerchief signal and waved a mini **ALBEMARLE FLAG**.

The **wolf cub** selling souvenirs saw the flag wave, put his paw to his muzzle and whistled.

A **raccoon** in a trilby, sitting at the edge of the platform, heard the whistle, folded his newspaper and stood up to go to the toilet.

The **skunk** on the platform nodded at the **raccoon** and stepped away from the trapdoor lever. He walked to the front of the platform, cleared his throat and announced to the waiting crowd: 'This particular execution is . . . postponed!'

Pelf was safe.

For now.

CHAPTER SEVEN

Dreadful Boredom Awaits Within This Chapter

After another charming bicycle ride through **CRUMBRIDGE**, we find ourselves on the broad avenue known as PICCALILLI, outside a quaint tea shop. At a table on the street an ancient marmoset lecturer mumbles something to a pretty student over afternoon tea. His **fanciful scientific theories** are lost on his young companion, who is distracted by the scone crumbs lodged in the professor's greying whiskers.

Now observe:

Next door to the tea shop is a bookshop. Not an unusual thing in **CRUMBRIDGE**. It has an unassuming front, the sort one might walk past every day and never really notice. Its sign, in faded and peeling gilt writing, details the shop's name. A name so mundane the signwriter fell asleep before finishing the job.

Dreary & Snores Antiquarian Books of Minor Interes

An unexpected setting for the next chapter of Mabel Jones's unlikely adventures, for surely **dreadful boredom** awaits us inside.

Or maybe . . .

Just maybe . . .

This unassuming shopfront hides a **secret**.

A very secret

secret indeed.

For if we were to **sneak** inside, making sure to smother the bell that hangs above the door . . .

If we were to quietly **creep** past the grey-suited, grey-faced grey goose that sits at his desk, rearranging his grey stationery by the glow of a flickering gaslight . . .

If we were to examine the **dusty bookshelf** in the **darkest corner** and observe that, among faded textbooks detailing the finer points of the sandwich industry, one book seems out of place: a worn-out copy of the popular classic

Arbuttle's I-Spy Mechanized Machines of Warfare . . .

And, if we were to reach for this book and pull it gently from the bookcase, we would hear . . .

A click.

A whirring.

And then a **clunk.**

And the bookcase would swing open to reveal a secret door to . . .

THE **TOP-SECRET**

HEADQUARTERS OF THE

ALBEMARLE **TOP-SECRET**

SERVICE, WHERE A

TOP-SECRET MEETING

IS ABOUT TO TAKE PLACE!

CHAPTER EIGHT

The Top-secret Headquarters of the Top-secret Service

For the attention of:

Sir Lockheed Beagle, Head of the Albemarle Top-secret Service

URGENT. Intercepted communications lead us to believe an enemy spy is operating in Albemarle. See attached file for details.

Regards, Springfeather

Name: Von Klaar

Species: Unknown

Details: All spies are familiar with the legend of the Alsatian master spy known as Von Klaar but no one has ever managed to reveal his true identity. Von Klaar is a master of disguise, skilled in many languages and a deadly assassin. He is ruthless in the face of danger and relentless in his mission to further the advancement of the Alsatian Empire, at the expense of our beloved Albemarle (God save the Queen!). **He should be approached with extreme caution.**

Mabel Jones snatched the file from Omynus Hussh's paw.

'I'm not sure we're supposed to be reading this,' she whispered, sliding it back into the filing cabinet. 'And *stop* taking things that aren't yours!'

Omynus Hussh hung his head in shame.

SIR LOCKHEED BEAGLE's secretary, an attractive young chicken by the name of Springfeather, looked up from his typewriter. He peered through thick lenses at the unlikely group before him.

'Sir Lockheed will see you now,' he said.

Sir Lockheed Beagle sat in a black leather chair behind a grand desk in a windowless wood-panelled office. He looked up as Mabel, Jarvis and Omynus entered.

'So, you are the famous Mabel Jones.'

Mabel Jones scratched her armpit.

'I'm *a* Mabel Jones. I'm not sure if I'm famous, though.'

Sir Lockheed smiled and his eyes twinkled.

'Well, I've heard of you. My sources say you and your . . . erm . . . **ASSOCIATES** are experienced adventurers, which is just what I need. I'm afraid, though, we can't release your other friend yet.'

Mabel frowned.

'But it's not fair! Pelf hasn't done anything.'

Sir Lockheed sighed. 'He was caught with enough tobacco to give a giraffe laryngitis. And he has a record of **PIRACY** as long as an elephant's trunk.'

He scratched behind a hairy ear.

'*However*, I might be able to pull a few strings, so to speak . . . But only if you will do something for me first.'

Mabel looked at Jarvis and Omynus. It didn't seem as if they had any choice.

'OK.'

Sir Lockheed clapped his paws together.

'Excellent! It's agreed. You help me and I'll have your friend set free!'

He took a photograph from a drawer and slid it across the desk towards Mabel.

Jarvis gasped.

'It's the convent!'

Sir Lockheed nodded.

'Indeed! We've had it under observation for some time. Who would believe such a humble place once contained something so **powerful** that the two greatest empires of our time would be in a deadly race to get it. Its name is –'

Outside, there was a flash of lightning, closely followed by a roll of thunder.

'Its name is the
DOOMSDAY BOOK!'

Sir Lockheed looked Mabel in the eyes as though trying to gauge her reaction.

'I believe you may have heard of it.'

Jarvis nodded.

'We have. We're –'

'Just interested in what happened to the hoomans,' interrupted Mabel, looking at Jarvis pointedly. She wasn't sure she wanted to let Sir Lockheed know that they were looking for the DOOMSDAY BOOK too.

'How can a book be powerful?' she asked Sir Lockheed.

He looked at her over the rim of his teacup.

'Knowledge *is* power, Mabel Jones. Our scientists

inform us that long ago an event happened that wiped the hooman species from this earth. The cause of that event is revealed within the pages of the DOOMSDAY BOOK!'

He shook his head.

'Imagine if that knowledge were to fall into the hands of the Alsatian Empire! And if they used it against our own great nation! What hope is there for the civilized world of **ALBEMARLE** in the face of such overwhelming power?'

'But the DOOMSDAY BOOK was taken from the convent years ago,' said Mabel.

Sir Lockheed stood up and walked over to a map on the wall. Taking a pencil from the breast pocket of his corduroy suit, he pointed at a city towards the bottom of the map.

'Have you heard of **Otom**?' he asked.

The three friends shook their heads.

Sir Lockheed's eyes twinkled. He sat back down at his desk and opened a small folder.

'According to legend, the **holy city of Otom** was founded nine hundred and ninety-nine years ago from the rubble of a ruined hooman city. It became a centre for learning. Indeed most of the great discoveries of our age can be traced back to Otomite scholars working in its **Grand Library**. Things we now take for granted: geometry, advanced mathematics, how jam gets in the middle of doughnuts. The list is endless.'

He paused briefly to open a biscuit tin.

'We believe this **Grand Library** is –'

Outside, there was a flash of lightning, closely followed by a roll of thunder.

'The final resting place of

THE
DOOMSDAY
BOOK!'

Jarvis scratched his head.

'So you want us to go and get it from the library?'

That didn't sound *too* difficult.

Sir Lockheed dipped a biscuit in his tea.

'Sadly, times have changed. Some years ago, the city fell under the rule of a creature named the **GRAND ZHOOL**.'

He bit the soggy part off the biscuit.

'An unsavoury character, by all accounts. He has an obsessive fear of **dirt**. The stuff drives him mad with fury – and he's been known to order the deaths of species he considers unclean: rats, cockroaches –'

Sir Lockheed removed a scruffy hankie from his pocket and wiped his whiskers.

'And **hoomans**.'

Mabel took a deep breath.

'Then why send *us* on this mission?'

Sir Lockheed smiled.

'Because it's the last thing the spies of the **Alsatian Empire** will expect! We believe their top agent is in **CRUMBRIDGE** at this very moment, seeking the very same book. His name is **VON KLAAR**.'

He fished a biscuit crumb from his tea with a corner of his hankie.

'Besides, this year is the one thousandth anniversary of the founding of **Otom**. Pilgrims from around the world will be visiting the city for the **FESTIVAL OF ST STATHAM**. There will be so many people coming and going that you should be able to go unnoticed if you're in disguise. It's perfect timing, don't you think?'

Sir Lockheed closed the file.

'This contains all the information you will need. You'll also be accompanied by our two finest spies. You can find them in the port of **SHRIMPWICH** – look for a fishing boat called the **Sunbeam** and await the signal.'

Mabel nodded. It seemed like quite a dangerous mission. She didn't know much about **wars** or **international espionage**, and it was strange to be taking sides in a conflict she knew nothing about. Still, if finding the book could help to free Pelf *and* save the hooman race, then why not?

Sir Lockheed grinned and pushed the folder across the desk towards Mabel.

'It's not much to ask in return for saving your friend from the creaking gibbet, is it?'

CHAPTER NINE
The Sunbeam

SHRIMPWICH, the principal port of **ALBEMARLE**, is the busiest harbour in the world. Along its many wharves lie passenger liners bound for the **NOO WORLD**, mackerel steamers arriving from the **FROZEN NORTH**, and the mighty frigates of the **ALBEMARLE NAVY**, all unloading or loading their cargo. Large mechanical cranes lift huge and heavy crates from the ships on to the docks. Usually a rowdy crowd of sailors fills the streets, spilling from the dockside taverns to fall prey to the shady trades of the local pickpockets and street hustlers.

Today, however, was different.

Today, war was on the horizon, and the streets were full of soldiers awaiting transport to foreign shores.

Moving through the crowds, Mabel Jones spotted a little boat moored between two gigantic

warships. A small hand-painted sign on its hull read Sunbeam.

The Sunbeam appeared to be a fishing boat. It had a cabin at the bow end and a winch at the stern. Attached to the winch was an old net, which was currently lying on the deck. The smell of rotten fish wafted up to Mabel and her friends.

It didn't look like the kind of vessel owned by the **ALBEMARLE TOP-SECRET SERVICE**.

But, then, I suppose that's the point.

'Do we really have to sail this all the way to **Otom** on our own?' asked Jarvis.

Mabel scratched her head.

'We've got their two best spies to help, remember.'

A small voice spoke from nearby.

''Scuse me, guv.'

Mabel looked down. A scruffy hedgehog in a stained, floppy sailor's cap looked up at her.

'Which one of you is Mabel Jones?' he asked.

Mabel eyed him suspiciously. She was on a **TOP-SECRET** mission, after all.

'Who wants to know?'

The hedgehog shrugged.

'No skin off my snout, mate. I just got a message for 'im.'

'And?' said Mabel.

The hedgehog looked around nervously.

'Sir Lockheed said you will receive furver instructions if you go an' stand over there, by those crates.'

He motioned with his head towards a pile of heavy crates on the dockside.

Mabel frowned.

'Why didn't he just get you to give me the instructions?'

The hedgehog smiled and winked.

'It's on a need-to-know basis, ain't it?'

Mabel shrugged and walked over to the crates.

'About here?' she shouted.

'Left a bit!' shouted the hedgehog.

'Here?'

'Bit more.'

'*Here?*'

'That'll do.'

Mabel picked her nose thoughtfully.

Am I just
supposed
to wait here?

While she waited, Mabel's mind wandered a little. The hedgehog seemed strangely familiar.

She was fairly sure there hadn't been a hedgehog in any of her *previous* unlikely adventures, but still . . . there was something about his eyes . . .

Suddenly the world seemed to darken, as if the sun had gone behind a cloud. Mabel shivered. Maybe **bad weather** was blowing in.

She looked up.

If that huge falling crate wasn't blocking the sky, she thought, *maybe I would be able to see if there's a storm –*

AND THEN IT HIT HER!

No, not the falling crate, but the realization that a falling crate was hurtling straight towards her at a speed that could only mean one thing:

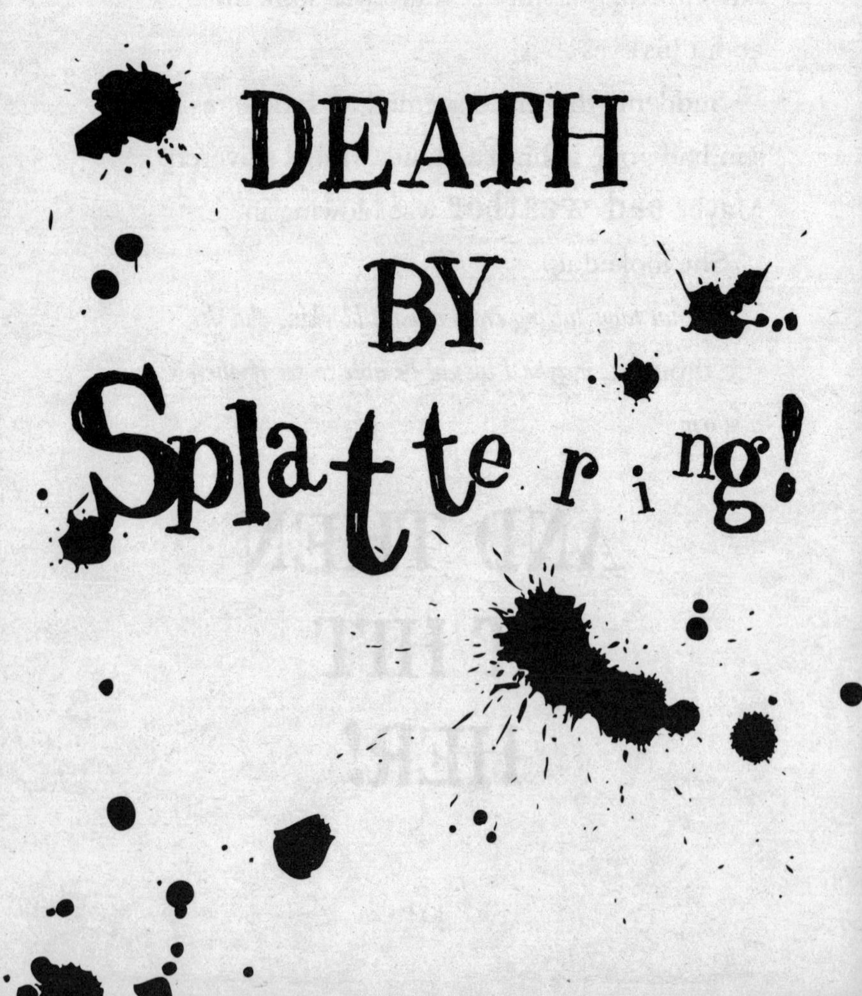

CHAPTER TEN

The Fur Coat of Righteousness

The sound of smart, confident footsteps echoes down the marble corridors of the **Grand Palace of Otom**. They belong to a black cat. A fancy-booted feline in a peacock-feathered cap and flamboyant trousers. He pauses before an ornate mirror, twirls, then bows politely to his own reflection.

'Looking radiant as always, **Eduardo**,' he says to himself, doffing his cap, before continuing on his way.

I recognize him, but *you* may not mingle amid

the A-list world of **INTERNATIONAL CELEBRITY**, so I brought a glossy magazine for you to peruse. There is bound to be some article or other about him.

Aha! Here's one:

The city of Gatto waves goodbye to the world's greatest artist, Eduardo, as he leaves to complete his most difficult commission yet: a portrait of the Grand Zhool of Otom.

Shamed MP caught in gambling scandal.

The clip-clopping shoes of Eduardo skip nearer and nearer the gilded and **ornately carved** double doors that lead to the chambers of the Grand Zhool.

Beneath his arm is a rolled canvas. A portrait of the Grand Zhool himself. After three months of hard work, today is its unveiling. This will be Eduardo's final visit to the Zhool's chambers.

But not for the reason he thinks.

An armed hyena, dressed in the plumed helmet and striped tunic of the **Grand Zhool's Personal Guard**, silently opens the doors to the chambers. A pale, wet-lipped gopher stands before him in a conical hat of purple velvet.

The gopher's eyes dart around the artist's face, as though looking for a flaw. But there is none. For Eduardo's handsomeness is second to none, as is his charming smile, which he now flashes at the gopher.

'Why, hello, **Govvel**.'

The gopher returns the smile with one of his own. But it is the opposite of charming. It is a false smile, accompanied by disdainful, disregarding, disrespectful eyes. He rubs his little hands together slowly. A small tongue pokes from his mouth to moisten his already wet lips.

'Have you got it?' he whispers.

Eduardo bows politely.

'Naturally, Govvel. My *masterpiece* is at last complete.'

Govvel stands aside.

'Then the Grand Zhool will grant you an audience.'

But who is this Grand Zhool? I hear you ask.

Who is this creature that lives deep within the bowels of the **Grand Palace of Otom**?

I'm afraid you shall very soon see.

A voice – deep, soft and wicked – speaks from behind a pair of lacy curtains.

'Who dares wake the Grand Zhool from his divine slumber?'

Eduardo gulps, his confidence suddenly drained by the voice of the Grand Zhool. Eduardo may be the world's leading artist, he may be feted in all the civilized cities in the world, he may own the world's third most expensive pair of pantaloons, but . . .

Even after all this, he is just an *artist*. A mere *doodler*. A pencil-toting, canvas-bothering **smudge-maker**. And it is well known that those with a leaning towards the arts are also cursed with the natural pale-kidneyed cowardliness that makes them unfit to appear in such stories as this.

Unfit to meet such

villainous evil

as we are about to witness.

Govvel bows so low his nose almost scrapes the floor.

'Your Grace, the portrait is finished.'

The lacy curtains slowly open and a massive grey hand appears, adorned with countless ruby rings. Govvel skips forward and, standing on his absolute tiptoes, takes the hand in his. He stretches up his furry face and gently kisses the fat fingers.

'Good morning, Your Grace,' he simpers.

Another massive grey hand appears, this one holding a silken flannel. The second hand wipes the first hand clean and then disappears. Finally the curtains open and, gently guided by the gopher, an obese hippopotamus steps out.

Huge rolls of **FAT** hang from his body, which is barely covered by the softest-looking of fur coats. On his head perches a spotless white skullcap.

IT IS THE GRAND ZHOOL!

He yawns. 'Has it captured my magnificence?'

Nervously Eduardo begins to unroll the painting. A bead of sweat drips from the end of his nose, and it is as though that tiny droplet contains his last millilitre of confidence.

He clears his throat nervously and begins to speak.

'Your Grace, it is a great honour to have finally finished your portrait, painted in the style of the ancient artists that lived in the time of the . . .'

Oh no! He's going to say it.

The Word.

THE DREADED WORD!

Oh, poor, beautiful Eduardo. If he'd only listened to the warning words of wisdom from his friends, who'd cautioned against such a trip to **Otom**.

He would have known that the word was **forbidden**, and that the mere **thought** of mentioning it in the presence of the Grand Zhool would lead him to an **untimely demise**.

But he hadn't listened. He was probably quaffing champagne at a posh party instead. Artists are like that.

And **the word . . .**

Alas, I cannot say it.

Not here.

Not now.

You wish to hear **the word?**

But we are also in the presence of His Grace, the Grand Zhool . . .

You insist?

Very well. Then sneak to the side and I will whisper it.

Eduardo spoke **the word . . .**

'HOOMANS!'

The Grand Zhool grimaces.

He presses a silken handkerchief to his mouth as though about to **vomit**. And then he fixes Eduardo with his heavy-lidded eyes.

'*Hoomans?* You dare mention hoomans to *me*? Even the mere mention of the word disgusts me.'

He motions to the artist.

'Come, Eduardo. Gaze from this window, over the city of **Otom**!'

The cat nervously approaches the window.

A beautiful city of whitewashed houses, domed towers, all trimmed neatly with gold and blue, lies spread before them. In the distance, the placid waters of the *Calm Blue Sea* sparkle in the morning sunlight.

The Grand Zhool smiles down at him.

'In a week's time, it will be the **FESTIVAL OF ST STATHAM**. One thousand years since St Statham himself washed up on these shores and raised the city as you see it now: an exquisite place built upon a bedrock of hooman filth and decay.'

The Grand Zhool's nostrils flare, as if he can smell the filth from nine hundred and ninety-nine years away. He presses his hands together as if in prayer.

'That such an elegant city could be built upon such **festering foundations** is tribute to the divine leadership of St Statham.'

Eduardo nods. If there is anything the artist understands, it is beauty. And the city of **Otom** is beautiful indeed.

The Grand Zhool turns to him.

'And now, on the eve of this great anniversary, you seek to sully his memory by bringing a portrait of me, the Grand Zhool, guardian of **Otom**, heir of St Statham, painted in the style of a **hooman**?! I had thought you a good cat, Eduardo, but perhaps I was mistaken.'

Eduardo falls to his knees. He is ignorant of many of the ways of the city of **Otom**, but he has heard of one thing.

One terrible thing.

'Not that, Your Gracefulwonderfulnesship. Please, anything but that!'

The Grand Zhool nestles his face into his collar and breathes in deeply.

Eduardo's eyes widen in horror as the Grand Zhool's coat twitches, flowing around his enormous belly almost as if it was alive . . .

It IS alive!

'It is not for me to pass sentence upon thee, Eduardo. Let the **Fur Coat of Righteousness** judge you . . .'

And, with these words, the Grand Zhool claps his hands together and something dreadful happens.

SOMETHING VERY DREADFUL INDEED!

CHAPTER ELEVEN
Death by Splattering

If **CRUMBRIDGE** is the brain of **ALBEMARLE**, then **SHRIMPWICH** is its beating heart. From here, culture, civilization and scones are dispatched to the empire's far-flung colonies. And in return come **tea**, **spices** and exceedingly heavy crates of **pickled gherkins**, one of which has broken free of its **suspiciously frayed ropes** as it is craned from the deck of the *SHE-HERRING*, high over the head of Mabel Jones.

KER**SMASH**

A **CRACK**

A **SCHLURP**

A TINK

A **BOINK!**

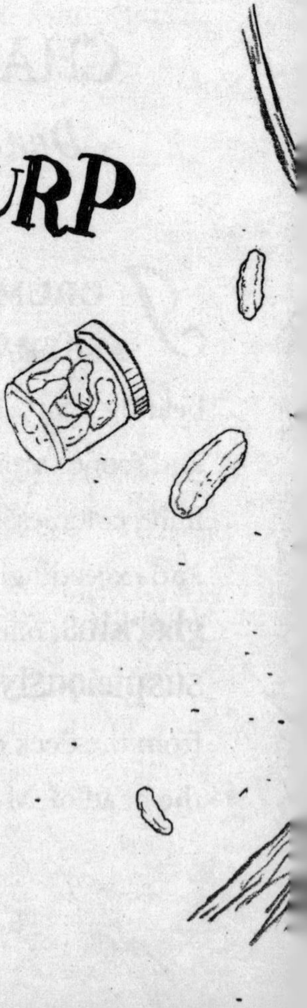

And, with that skilfully written sound, the crate crashed to the ground – exactly where Mabel Jones would have been had she not just leapt clear of its path. Splinters of wood and glass exploded across the docks, while a stray gherkin smacked Mabel Jones sharply on the side of her head, whereupon everything went black.

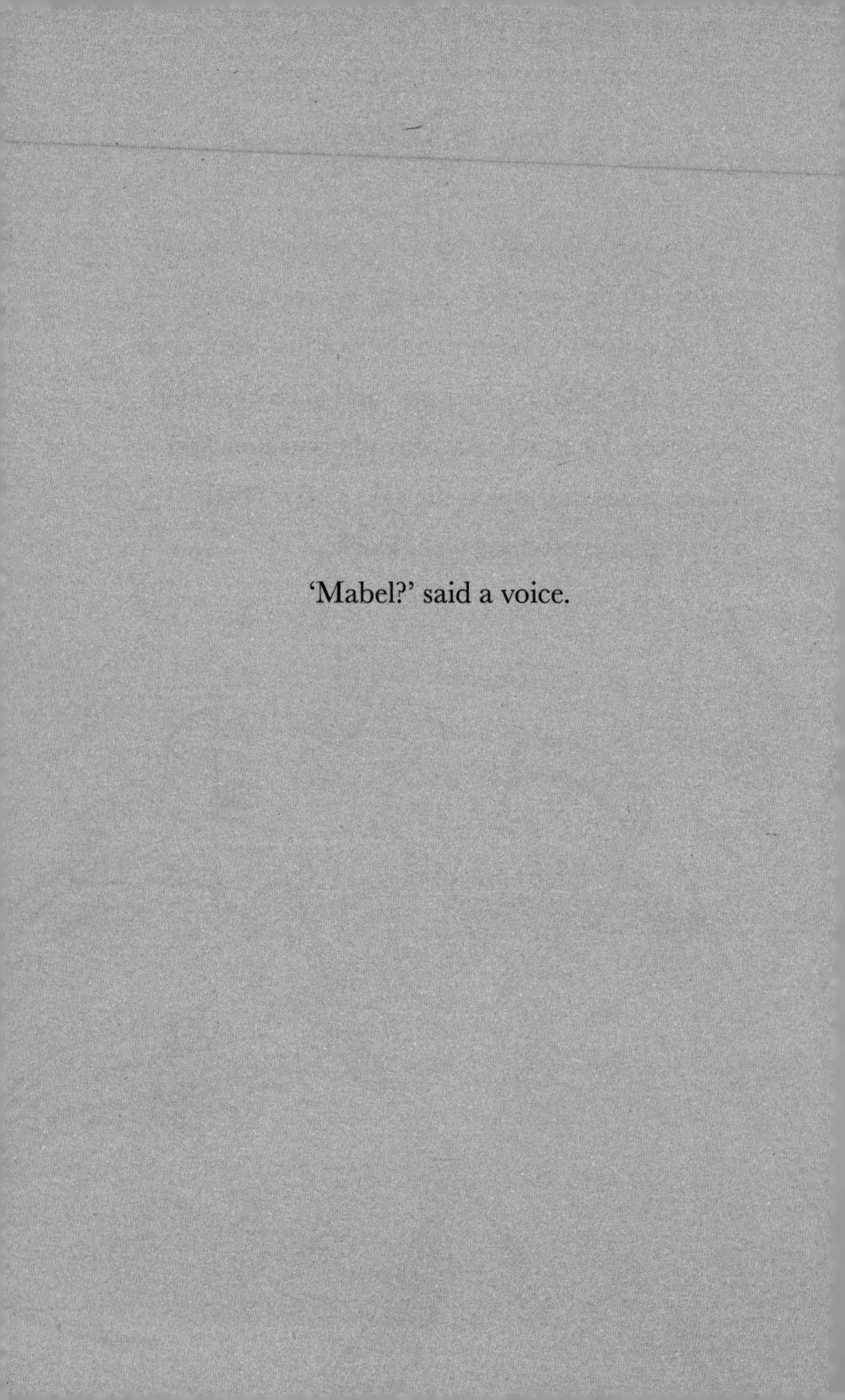
'Mabel?' said a voice.

'Child, are you all right?'

Mabel Jones forced open her eyes.

The docks seemed to spin around her.

She sat up and rubbed her head.

A penguin was kneeling by her side.

No, not a penguin – a nun! And not just any nun. It was the bulgy-eyed rabbit from ST HILDA'S CONVENT, Sister Miriam!

Jarvis came running up.

'That hedgehog tried to kill you!'

'Hedgehog?' said Sister Miriam. 'What hedgehog?'

They looked around, but the hedgehog was gone.

'I'm sure it was an accident,' twittered Sister Miriam. 'The rope must have snapped. You've had a very lucky escape!'

Jarvis scratched his head. 'I dunno. It *definitely* seemed like the hedgehog wanted you to stand just there.'

Sister Miriam looked at him sharply. 'It is

not our place to judge others, young man. The important thing is that Mabel is safe now.'

'What are *you* doing here, Sister Miriam?' Mabel asked.

Sister Miriam smiled.

'I am on a **pilgrimage**.'

'What's a pilgrimage?' asked Omynus Hussh.

Sister Miriam patted the loris on the head.

'It's a special and important journey. One week from today is the anniversary of the founding of the city of **Otom** by St Statham the Lion.'

'St Statham the Lion?' asked Jarvis. 'Who's he?'

Sister Miriam pulled out a small black book and carefully opened it.

In a

SOLEMN VOICE

she began

to read:

45. Lo, and so it was that St Statham the Lion, during a vacation, was thrown into the sea by treacherous gravy merchants.

46. Whereupon he felt great sadness in his abandonment until a flying seagull did appear unto him.

47. And St Statham swam towards the seagull until he reached a shore rich with marble and gold.

48. Whereupon he cast his dressing-gown to the sand and spake thus:

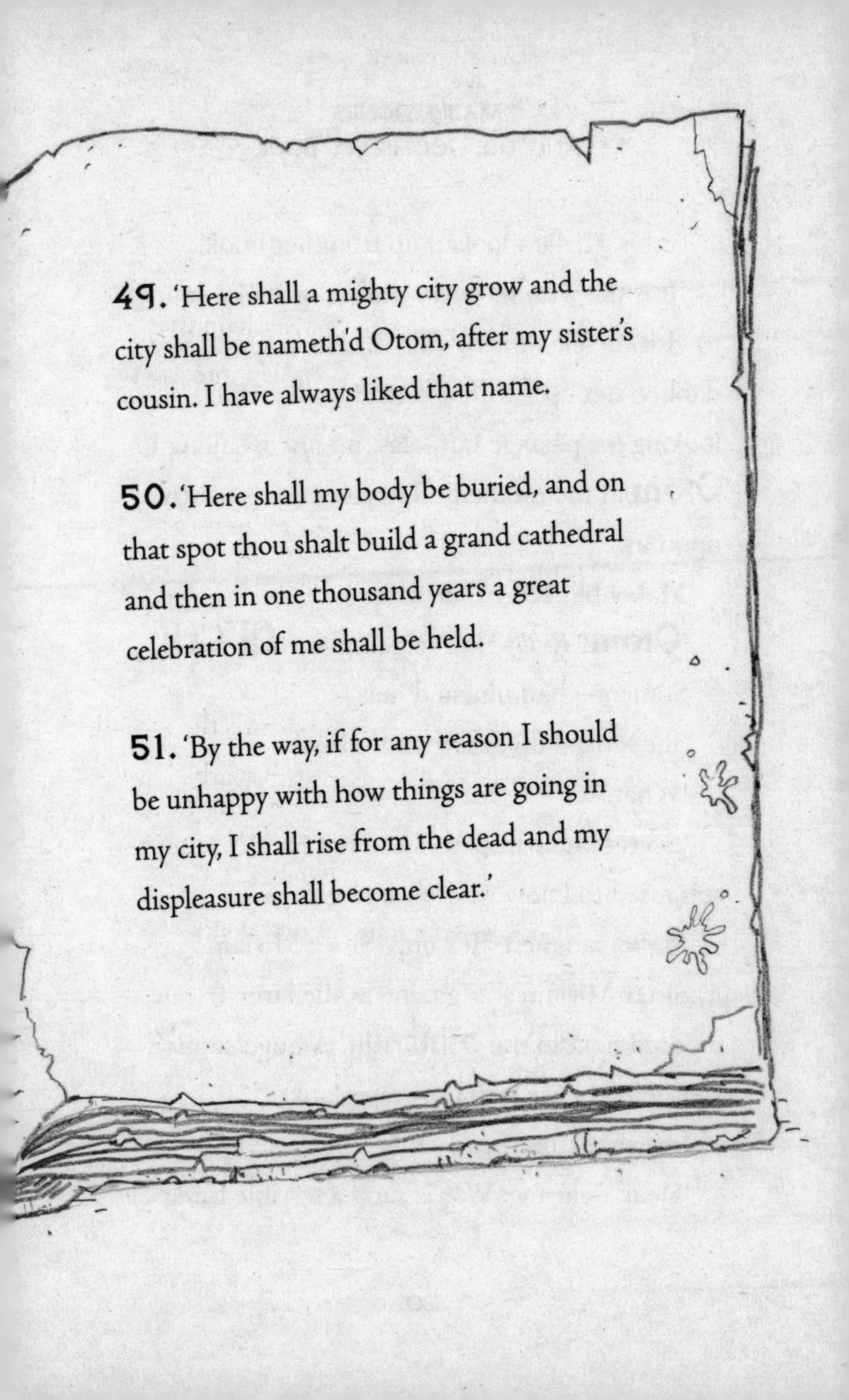

49. 'Here shall a mighty city grow and the city shall be nameth'd Otom, after my sister's cousin. I have always liked that name.

50. 'Here shall my body be buried, and on that spot thou shalt build a grand cathedral and then in one thousand years a great celebration of me shall be held.

51. 'By the way, if for any reason I should be unhappy with how things are going in my city, I shall rise from the dead and my displeasure shall become clear.'

Sister Miriam looked up from her book.

'It is the wish of every nun to be lucky enough to visit the city during this very holy time.' She dabbed her eyes with a worn handkerchief. 'I was looking for passage but, alas, no one is sailing to **Otom** at the moment. They say *war* is nearly upon us.'

Mabel blinked in surprise.

'**Otom!** *Really?* We're going to – **OUCH!**'

Someone had pinched her.

She looked up at Omynus Hussh.

'What?'

'Secret!' he whispered into her ear. 'No one's supposed to know where we're goings.'

Mabel laughed. 'It's only Sister Miriam.'

Sister Miriam was gazing at the large frigate moored next to the **Sunbeam**. A huge cannon was being heaved up the gangplank.

She shook her head sadly.

'Dear, dear me. War is such a terrible thing.

I wonder how many of these brave sailors will never see their loved ones again.'

She looked at Omynus.

'It's a terrible thing, missing your family, little loris.' Omynus flinched as she touched him gently on the cheek. 'I haven't seen my brother Jim for years. Not since he –'

She put her hand to her mouth to conceal a sob.

Jarvis shuffled awkwardly and Mabel put a comforting hand on Sister Miriam's shoulder.

'It's OK, Sister Miriam. We're going to **Otom**. We can take you there!' She looked around carefully to ensure she wouldn't be overheard. 'I have to warn you, though. We are on a **TOP-SECRET** and **VERY DANGEROUS** mission! We're just waiting for the last two members of the team.'

Jarvis looked at the **Sunbeam**. The little boat gently bobbed against the harbour wall.

'Do you think they're in there?' he asked.

And, as though to answer his question, a lamp was lit inside the **Sunbeam**. Then the light blinked. Three times!

'A signal!' cried Mabel.

Jarvis nodded excitedly.

'Yes. And, judging by how important Sir Lockheed thinks this mission is, they are probably the best spies in **ALBEMARLE**. Probably the best spies in the world!'

Mabel looked at the **Sunbeam**. The light flickered slightly and suddenly got brighter. Then it started moving around very rapidly.

'I think they're trying to send us some kind of message.'

'Is it Morse code?' asked Jarvis.

Then a loud voice boomed out from inside:

'Good heavens, *Speke*! You've set fire to my jacket!'

A hatch on top of the boat was flung open and a **BURNING BADGER** leapt out and into the sea.

'*Awfully* sorry, CARRUTHERS, old chap,' said an otter, appearing through the hatch. Then he stopped and stared at the three friends and Sister Miriam on the harbourside.

'I say! It's Mabel Jones and the gang!' he cried. 'What a delight! Carruthers, Carruthers!
Look who it is:
Mabel Jones!'

If you have read the second of Mabel Jones's unlikely adventures, you may recognize this pair: Professor Carruthers Badger-Badger, PhD, a respected scientist, and his loyal friend, Sir Timothy Speke, artist and poet.

Carruthers clambered slowly back on to the boat.

'Hello, young Mabel,' he said, brushing water from his coat. 'It seems Sir Lockheed took our recommendation and recruited you. So the old team is back together, and just in time. We have a **TOP-SECRET** mission to undertake.'

He knowingly tapped his little black nose.

'I'm afraid we cannot divulge the details –'

Speke nodded. 'Absolutely not. Not even to say that we've been sent to find something before it falls into enemy hands.'

Carruthers glared at his friend.

'Shh. You never know who may be listening. Loose lips sink ships, and all that.'

'Why, I didn't even mention the twist,' protested Speke, adjusting his monocle. 'The thing we're looking for is actually a **book**! Who would've believed it?!'

Carruthers frowned.

'Really, Speke! You are an **insufferable nitwit**! Von Klaar could be nearby. He is a master of disguise!'

Speke readjusted his monocle and peered about the busy dock.

'Curse that villainous Von Klaar! He too is on the trail of the DOOMSDAY BOOK. It's a race between the forces of good and evil!' He looked at Mabel. 'We're the goodies, obviously! Ha ha!'

Mabel smiled. Speke and Carruthers had shown themselves to be worthy friends. They might want to find the DOOMSDAY BOOK for different reasons from her, but she was still pleased they were on the same side.

Carruthers beckoned them down on to the deck of the Sunbeam.

'Yes, time is against us. A great war is on the horizon and the future of the world is at stake.' He looked grimly out to sea. 'We leave on the morning tide!'

'After a light breakfast of toast and marmalade!' added Speke.

And, with those thrilling words, the chapter ended.

Except it didn't.

Not for everyone.

Somewhere on the **Sunbeam**, skulking shyly in the shadows, slim and silent fingers are rifling through a handbag.

Sister Miriam's handbag!

What devious thievery is this?

The creature's whiskers twitch.

Some fur that grows in the wrong direction on top of his head is anxiously straightened with a licked paw.

'Omynus Hussh!'

It was Mabel Jones, and she was looking cross.

'How could you, Omynus?'

Omynus gulped and covered his head with his paw and doorknob.

'I . . . I . . . I just wanted to check somethings. Is you angry with me, snuglet?'

'I'm not angry, Omynus,' said Mabel,

taking back Sister Miriam's handbag. 'I'm just **disappointed**.'

Mabel frowned. She didn't have time to keep checking Omynus wasn't stealing stuff. They were about to begin a **MISSION**.

A very **DANGEROUS MISSION** indeed.

CHAPTER TWELVE
The Alsatian Ironclad

Dearest, sweetest Nanny Mimsy,

How I remember that long and glorious summer afternoon. I stood on tippy-toes and watched through the nursery window as Mother took refreshment on the lawn. What a woman – the kind of mother one could only ever dream of having.

'To your room, Timothy! I am sick of the sight of your pathetic mooning face,' she would scold fondly, giving me a loving cuff round the back of the head.

Ever the sensitive soul, I think I may have been weeping. You sat me on your knee and sang me a song – the tale of a soldier leaving his sweetheart – while I chewed thoughtfully upon a rusk. You gave me something. Do you remember? Daddy's medal.

Poor Daddy. I wish I'd known him. You said you'd found it on the floor in the shed. I suppose Mummy had put it there for safekeeping while she expanded their wardrobe into my bedroom to make space for more of her gowns. (She was so very glamorous, wasn't she?)

I've kept it safe ever since. First throughout the days and nights boarding at St Crispin's School for the Exceedingly Rich, then at university, where I met my chum Carruthers. If I had known that one day I, Sir Timothy

Speke, would be following in Daddy's footsteps, how my childish whiskers would have bristled with pride.

For you see, Mimsy, I have been recruited by the Albemarle Top-Secret Service. It seems that talks to calm the waters over Princess Helga's blow-off have collapsed and left us on the brink of a great war with those Alsatian brutes. I am to be sent on a top-secret mission – the details of which I cannot divulge (not even to tell you we are sailing to Otom). I certainly can't tell you about our search for the Doomsday Book, lest this letter fall into the paws of the dreaded enemy spy Von Klaar.

For now, though, all is calm. A thick fog has drifted across the sea and our little vessel has come to a halt until the fog clears and we can safely continue on our way south. This may be the last you hear of me, but don't be sad. Know that I have lived a full and happy life, and that if I am to die on this mission then I die for the honour of our great nation.

God save the Queen!

All my love,

Timmy

PS I sent the usual parcel of dirty laundry. I'll pick it up upon my return. The trousers will need pressing.

Sure enough, as is common at this time of year, a thick mist had fallen upon the sea, wrapping the Sunbeam in a cold dampness that chilled the livers of each and every member of the crew. After some discussion, Mabel Jones had decided to drop sail for fear that they might run aground on the treacherously rocky coast of SCRAPE. The crew huddled around the soft heat of a whale-fat lamp and waited.

And waited.

And waited.

Speke adjusted his monocle and smiled at the assembled bunch.

'I could recite a poem,' he suggested. 'To cheer the mood? It's a work in progress . . .'

The crew looked at one another. They had heard Speke's poetry before. To say that it was the **worst poetry ever written in the history of the world** would be unkind.

Unkind but true. Listen . . .

We wandered 'mongst the peach trees,
I smothered her with kisses,
And held her in my paws once more,
Caressed her golden whiskers.

He paused to wipe a tear from his eye.

'It's already moving stuff, no?' he said to Mabel, who nodded politely.

'I've got plenty more,' he added. 'If you'd like to hear?'

And, on that spectacularly **awkward** note, let us take our leave from this scene, for surely nothing of interest will happen this night. Nothing of the slightest interest at all . . .

WAIT!

What's that noise?

Do you hear it?

It's getting **louder!**

Yes. A dull groan sounds through the fog. A deadened creaking. The sound of ***huge steel cables*** stretched under a great weight. The sound of GREAT IRON PLATES contracting under the pressure of the cold sea. A mournful symphony of machinery and metal.

It grows even louder.

Carruthers frowned into the dense fog.

'I've got a very bad feeling about this.'

And, at the very moment he reached the full stop at the end of that sentence, they saw it.

Looming from the grey mist, a giant grey hulk. Dull grey waves lapped against dull grey iron – a ship so large its deck and stern disappeared into the fog.

Carruthers turned to face Mabel. His striped brow creased with panic.

'Dim the lights!' he hissed. 'It's an **Alsatian battlecruiser**!'

Mabel hid the lamp from sight.

And just in time.

'I'm sure I heard something, **Klinker**,' snarled a voice, its owner hidden high above in the thick fog.

'Ah, you're always hearing things, **Smutz** . . .'

The voice called Smutz growled.

'I don't want them to slip through on our watch. We have received information that the **ALBEMARLE** agents are already on their way to **Otom**. Curse this fog!'

Far below, on the deck of the **Sunbeam**,

Mabel Jones frowned.

'Albemarle agents'?
Do they mean . . . us?

'Ha! They wouldn't dare try to break through our lines. Our guns can sink an **ALBEMARLE FRIGATE** with a single shot!'

The voice called Smutz grunted in grudging agreement.

'But a coded message from Von Klaar has spoken of a boat called the *Sunbeam*.'

Mabel gasped.

THEY DO MEAN US!

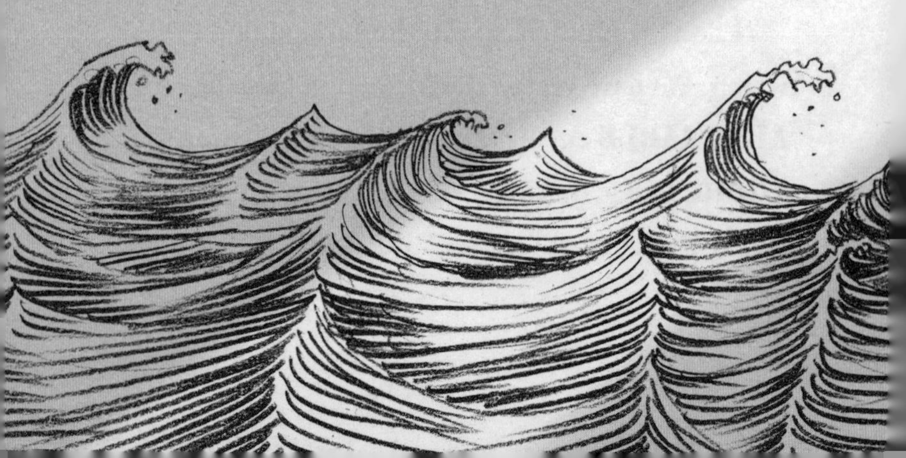

The crew of the **Sunbeam** looked at each other in horror. The fearsome **Alsatian Navy** was hunting for them! Their mission had already been compromised!

Powerful searchlights shone through the mist, sweeping across the waves and missing the **Sunbeam** by inches.

'You're wasting your time!' growled the voice belonging to Klinker. 'No ship could sneak past our navy. Not even in this fog!'

Mabel smiled. For once, the fog had been their friend, its cold and clammy embrace hiding them from their enemy. As long as they kept quiet and –

CLANNGGGG!

The crew turned round to see Sister Miriam standing over a dropped biscuit tin.

'Oh dearie me, I'm sorry. I was just about to offer the digestives round . . .'

Carruthers glared at the rabbit.

'This is no time for tea and biscuits! Why, it's not even eleven o'clock.'

Behind her, Omynus Hussh narrowed his saucery eyes, but just as he opened his mouth to say something a voice sounded from high above.

'Did you hear that, Klinker?'

'You're imagining things, I tell you – the sea plays funny tricks with your mind. I warned you not to have that third glass of **Wasp Rot** . . .'

Slowly the gruff and growling voices faded into the fog as the vast battlecruiser drifted past.

Once the only sound was the slap of waves against their own boat, Carruthers let out a long sigh and marked their position on a map.

'Never before has the **Alsatian battle fleet** dared to venture so far into **ALBEMARLE** waters.' He shook his head. 'Things look bleaker than ever.'

Mabel nodded. So much depended on their mission. All they had to do was find a book.

It sounded easy.

But these things never are.

Arbuttle's Guide
Otom
Where even the weather is blessed!
Otom
UPDATED EDITION

The Grand Cathedral of St Statham
Take a stroll through the charming alleyways and avenues to the Grand Cathedral of St Statham, built from marble and gold in honour of St Statham. Remember to wipe your feet before entering.*

The Grand Palace
Every Sunday the Grand Zhool appears to his followers from a balcony overlooking the main square. Make sure to get there early for a splendid view of His Holy Gracefulness. And also remember to not catch his eye.*

The Grand Library
Browse the limitless bookshelves and immerse yourself in the rich history of the world in the Grand Library of Otom, the largest collection of books in the civilized world.

* Offenders will be judged by the Fur Coat of Righteousness.

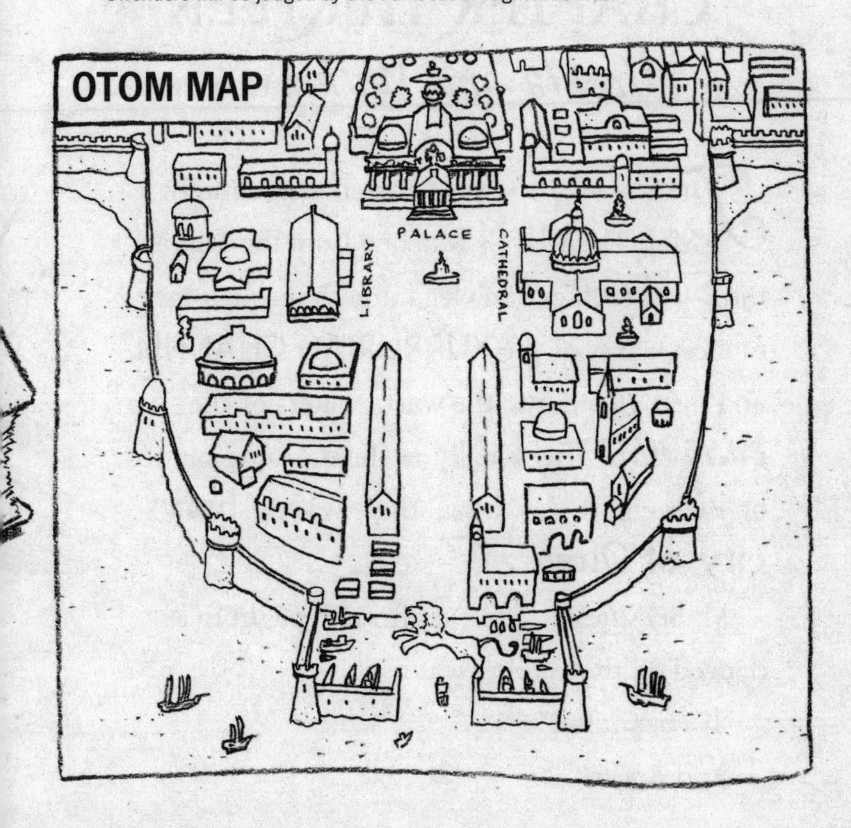

CHAPTER THIRTEEN
Ursula and Wilkinson

The rest of the voyage passed uneventfully. Mabel and Jarvis watched from the rails as the *Sunbeam* cut an elegant path through the modest waves of the YURRUPIAN CHANNEL and then glided into the warm waters of the *Calm Blue Sea*. Finally, as the morning sun rose on their eighth day at sea, there was the **holy city of Otom**.

Mabel shielded her eyes from the light that danced off the lapping waters.

'It's beautiful!'

And it was.

Towers of marble rose from perfectly whitewashed walls. The huge pointed dome of the GRAND CATHEDRAL OF ST STATHAM sparkled in the sun and reflected turquoise and gold across the city. And, bestriding the entrance to the quayside, there was a giant statue of a **rampant lion**, his front paws raised in defiance of any foe that dared attack his city.

Sister Miriam laughed a joyful and tinkling laugh.

'St Statham the Lion!' She pressed her hands together in joy. 'He's just as I always imagined!'

The harbour was packed with boats large and small. Passenger ferries from YURRUP, merchantmen from the SLIGHTLY FURTHER NEAR EAST, but mainly sail upon sail of smaller vessels, all jostling for position. On the shore, crowds of pilgrims bustled about with luggage, and a smartly uniformed tapir was climbing down a ladder into a small rowing boat.

Carruthers looked at Mabel.

'It's the harbourmaster coming to help us dock. He'll be checking we don't have any banned cargo aboard too.'

Mabel blinked.

'And do we?'

'Just you and Jarvis,' replied Carruthers. 'Which is why we have this for you to hide in.'

He pointed to a large barrel labelled HALIBUT.

Mabel took the lid from the barrel.

'It's full of rotten fish!'

Carruthers smiled and reached inside the barrel.

'Aha! You reckon without the ingenuity of the **ALBEMARLE TOP-SECRET SERVICE**! This is a false top with rotten fish stuck on. It conceals a hidden chamber underneath . . .'

He rummaged his paw around, then pulled the false top from the barrel with a proud smile.

'There is *also* a secret door in the back that can

only be opened from the inside and a small knothole to peer through.'

Mabel looked gingerly into the cramped confines of the barrel.

It was dark.

It smelt of fish.

Jarvis screwed his nose up.

They looked at each other

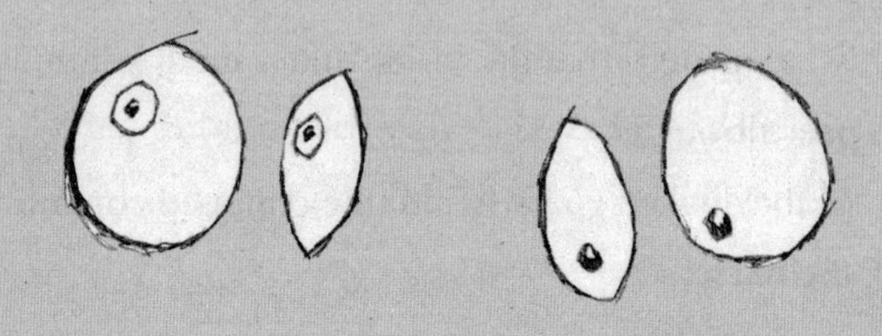

It's hard to stay hidden in a whiffy barrel.

Mabel and Jarvis kept very still and very quiet until they felt the Sunbeam bump against the dock.

'It stinks in here,' whispered Jarvis.

'Shh!' hissed Mabel. 'I'm trying to see.'

She pressed her eye to the hole in the barrel. Out on the dockside, a crowd was gathering. A familiar bulging-eyed nun was among them.

'There's Sister Miriam!' Mabel hissed. 'She must be having a look around.'

Mabel could hear the harbourmaster explaining to Speke and Carruthers what was happening.

'It is the celebration of ST STATHAM'S SEAGULL, where an offering is made to the sacred seagull in thanks for the safe guidance of St Statham to these shores. You are very lucky travellers, for you are about to behold the Grand Zhool himself!'

As the harbourmaster spoke, a procession began to wind its way down to the waterfront. Mabel saw the street cleaners first. Armed with buckets and mops, they were **furiously** scrubbing the already spotless pavements as if their lives depended upon it.

Next came a group of soldiers, resplendent in the blue-and-yellow-striped tunics of the Grand Zhool's Personal Guard.

Then, finally, an ornate domed carriage – the size of a large beach hut – hoisted upon two thick poles carried on the **sweating shoulders** of twenty pigs, five on each corner. On the top of this carriage a sunken-faced, wet-lipped gopher sat upon a small chair.

As the carriage reached the waterside, the gopher stood and waved his hand.

The sweaty pigs stopped, and slowly and painfully dropped to their knees.

The gopher climbed down a silver ladder and

opened a door in the side of the carriage, and the obese form of the Grand Zhool stepped out, a handkerchief pressed to his face. He glared around at the crowd and slowly walked to the water's edge.

Carefully he took a **golden box** from his fur coat and opened it, emptying some breadcrumbs into his fat hand.

He looked out towards the *Calm Blue Sea* and began to speak, his booming voice repeating the same verses that Mabel had read from Sister Miriam's book:

'Lo, and so it was that St Statham the Lion, during a vacation, was thrown into the sea by treacherous gravy merchants. Whereupon he felt great sadness in his abandonment until a flying seagull did appear unto him. And St Statham swam towards the seagull until he reached a shore rich with marble and gold.'

The Grand Zhool paused and flung the breadcrumbs in the air.

'And, with these breadcrumbs, we thank thee, Seagull!'

The crowd cheered enthusiastically, keeping their eyes on the sky. Clearly there was more to come!

Our position in the crow's-nest of the yacht berthed next to the Sunbeam allows us the perfect view.

See there, hidden at the back of the crowd, a wizened whippet with tired and baggy eyes watches the scene from beneath a flat cap. The whippet's name is Wilkinson. For ten years he has been training *Ursula*, his pet seagull, for this very moment. Taking her gently from her cage, he tenderly kisses her beak.

Then he fastens her **tutu** with a neat bow. 'We wouldn't want it slipping off, Ursula, would we? Not on our **big day**. Now, remember what we've practised. Land, curtsy, then fly off.'

And, as the Grand Zhool's breadcrumb offering drifted in the wind, Wilkinson threw Ursula into the air.

Ursula flew high and out above the sea, then circled round to land gracefully at the Grand Zhool's feet.

The Grand Zhool turned to the crowd.

'Behold! St Statham has sent us his **sacred seagull**!'

The crowd clapped politely.

Ursula made a perfect curtsy.

The Grand Zhool raised his hands to the sky.

'Behold! The seagull has shown its deference to me, the Grand Zhool!'

Ursula turned round and prepared to fly off.

At the back of the crowd, Wilkinson removed his cap and wiped the sweat from his wrinkled brow. His life's work was complete. It was

notoriously hard training seagulls, but he had done it.

No. He shook his head. *They* had done it. Him *and* Ursula. Together.

Then it happened.

Just as she left the ground . . .

Just as she prepared to make her triumphant flight back out to sea . . .

Just as the Grand Zhool was preparing to leave . . .

Ursula did what seagulls do best.

The Grand Zhool looked down in horror at his **poo-spattered feet**.

He turned to Govvel.

'Fetch the seagull trainer!' he boomed.

Inside the barrel, Mabel Jones felt Jarvis wriggle uncomfortably.

'I can't see,' he whispered. 'Let me have a turn.'

Mabel kept her eye to the hole. She had a feeling something **dreadful** was about to occur. Maybe it was better if Jarvis didn't see.

The Grand Zhool glared at the crowd as it parted to make way for Wilkinson the whippet. He was held firmly between two of the Grand Zhool's Personal Guard.

They threw him to the hard stone floor of the dock.

The Grand Zhool's face grew dark with rage.

He looked at the cowering form of the wizened whippet.

'You've made me look a fool, Wilkinson.'

Wilkinson looked up at the raging hippo.

'Please, Your Grace . . . not the coat. Anything but that!'

The hippo scowled.

Mabel blinked. His fur coat seemed to be **moving**. ***Writhing***. Small paws were appearing. Little snouts sniffing . . .

Sniffing for **FEAR**.

And then something dreadful **did** happen.

Something very dreadful indeed.

Parts of the fur coat seemed to spring to life, peeling away from the white silken lining. They moved so fast it was hard for Mabel to make out what kind of animal they were – a blur of ripping claws and biting teeth.

Then she realized. The coat was made of weasels!

Ferocious,

blood-crazed

weasels!

Mabel turned her face away from the peephole as they leapt upon Wilkinson.

'It's horrible!' she cried. 'That poor whippet!'

Then, after bracing herself for a moment, she pressed her eye to the peephole again.

The Grand Zhool's carriage was making its way back through the horrified crowd.

On the dockside, a lonely seagull in a neatly tied tutu stood looking at a bloodstained flat cap.

Of Wilkinson, there was no other sign.

CHAPTER FOURTEEN
Maniacal Pigeon Fever

Night has crept across the great city of **Otom** and all is silent except for the clanking silver breastplates of the patrolling Grand Zhool's Personal Guard. It is forbidden to wander the city after dark, but we are safely hidden in the pigeon loft of the old pizzeria, which provides an excellent view of the **Grand Plaza** and the **Grand Library**.

Focus your binoculars on the doors of the **Grand Library**. Read its words with dread:

CLOSED

FOR ALL ETERNITY

BY ORDER OF THE GRAND ZHOOL

FOR THE CRIME OF LENDING BOOKS

OF AN UNCLEAN NATURE,

BEING BY OR UPON THE SUBJECT OF HOOMANS.

TRESPASSERS WILL BE JUDGED BY THE

FUR COAT OF RIGHTEOUSNESS.

The patrol has passed from sight. All is quiet. Quiet apart from –

Would you mind stopping that scratching? It puts me off my narrative somewhat.

What do you mean, you *itch*?

Oh, those. Ignore those. That is just the mostly harmless bite of the **common pigeon louse**. Your hair is probably infested by now.

Nothing that a shaven head won't cure. Only one in five fleas actually carries the **MANIACAL PIGEON FEVER** anyway.

Me?

Oh, they don't bother me. I always bring **louse repellent** on such unlikely adventures as these, especially after I picked up an annoying dose of **sea nits** from the sofa in the CADAVEROUS LOBSTER TAVERN. It took ages combing them from my buttock-fur.

Anyway, we are not here to discuss my medical problems. I suggest you keep your personal questions to yourself.

But what is this?

A movement among the shadows?

Pass me the binoculars . . .

Yes. Five figures lurk suspiciously. And rightly so, for they are out and about beyond the hour of the Grand Zhool's curfew. Who are these mysterious figures?

They scamper across the moonlit plaza to an alleyway that leads alongside the locked and forgotten **Grand Library of Otom**.

Hark! The sound of breaking glass! A burglary is about to occur!

We should join it.

Of all the dangerous deeds ever perpetrated in the course of an unlikely adventure, this must surely be the most foolhardy: Mabel and Jarvis, both **FORBIDDEN** creatures, entering a **FORBIDDEN** building, to search for a **FORBIDDEN** book.

And all **FORBIDDEN** by order of the Grand Zhool himself!

Outside the library waits Sir Timothy Speke. He is half keeping watch and half trying to free Carruthers Badger-Badger, who is wedged in a small window.

'It's not that you're **FAT**, Carruthers, just that the window is too small,' explains Speke as he pulls on his unfortunate friend's legs.

Inside the library, Mabel Jones wipes the dust from a sign on a nearby door.

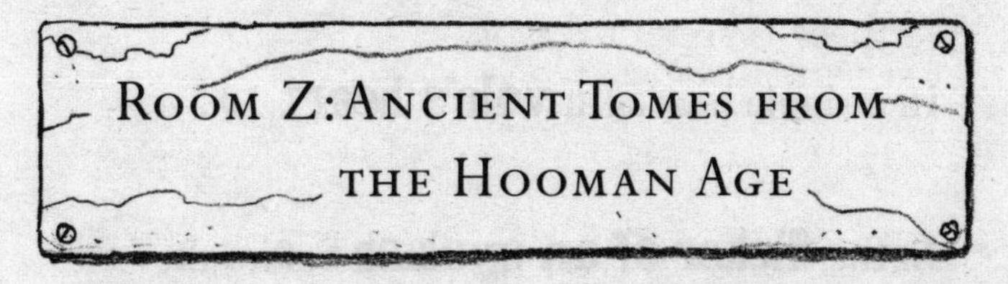

She turns to Jarvis, who is dawdling behind, leafing through a book of music with Omynus Hussh.

'I used to play music once,' mutters Jarvis. 'In the old days.'

Mabel sighs. Sometimes she forgets that Jarvis must miss his old life in the past as much as she misses hers.

'Come on, you two,' she says gently.

But Jarvis isn't listening. His head is deep in the book.

He doesn't notice that, behind Mabel's back, the door to Room Z has swung open, revealing **pure darkness** beyond . . .

He doesn't see, at that **very moment . . .**

In a single beat of a **vole's heart . . .**

In the **flicker of an eyelash** before the **blinking of an eye . . .**

In the **fraction of a second** that ends as soon as it begins . . .

THE LONG, BONY FINGERS OF A COLD, HAIRY HAND REACH FROM THE ROOM AND PULL HER INTO THE MUSTY DARKNESS!

Mabel Jones starts to scream, but no sound escapes as another similarly **cold and hairy** hand clamps round her mouth.

She hears the closing of the door and the turning of a key.

'Hello,' croaks a voice so close to her face she can almost feel the creature's whiskery lips brushing against her ear.

'I've been so lonely.'

CHAPTER FIFTEEN
The Librarian

In the darkness, Mabel Jones felt her feet leave the ground. She struggled uselessly against the creature's tight embrace.

Now she was high above the floor. The creature that held her leapt through the darkness with great agility until it stopped suddenly, and Mabel felt herself being carefully lowered on to a shelf. The hand that was clamped round her mouth was slowly released.

'My name is Mabel Jones and I'm not –'

'Shhhhhh!' said a voice, and Mabel felt a finger pressed against her lips.

There was the sound of a match being struck. A small flame illuminated the darkness. Then a larger flame appeared as a candle was lit. Mabel looked at the creature that sat beside her on the top bookshelf.

It was a grey and grizzled **gibbon** with long, matted hair. No wonder it had swung through the library with such ease. He had a strange expression on his face, half sad and half wild. But that might have been because his eyes looked in two different directions at once.

Mabel looked him in the eye closest to her – the sad one.

'Hello. I'm Mabel Jones,' she said.

The gibbon jerked his head to the side and looked at her through his madder eye.

'Shhh!'

Mabel reached out for the identification card that hung on a lanyard round his neck.

'You're a librarian,' said Mabel. 'But the library has been closed for **years**. You haven't been here all that time, have you? On your own?'

The gibbon raised a long arm and proudly gestured around the room with his long hand.

'My books!'

He bounced on his haunches and hooted excitedly.

Mabel looked about and her heart sank. As far as the candlelight reached, all she could see were rows upon rows of empty bookcases.

'Where are they all?'

Leonard's shoulders sank and he swivelled his head to fix her with his sad eye.

'Zhool came for hooman books. Hooman books all burnt.' He made a silent hooting face, then distractedly picked a small beetle from his fur and chewed it.

'All of them?' asked Mabel. She couldn't believe that she had come all the way to **Otom** only to find that the DOOMSDAY BOOK had been destroyed.

'Except one!' Leonard bounced excitedly on his haunches again. 'He never find that one. Leonard reserved the best one!'

Mabel held her breath. 'Which one?'

Leonard laughed a hooting laugh, then stopped suddenly. 'The book I reserved is called . . .'

He paused and, if **Otom** was the sort of place to get thunderstorms, then Mabel would've heard the distant sound of thunder.

'THE DOOMSDAY BOOK!'

He giggled again.

'Where is it now?' asked Mabel. 'Can you show it to me?'

'Oh no,' replied Leonard. 'Book smuggled from library under jumper and hidden away.'

He put his fingers to his lips and moved his face close to hers, his **wild whiskers** brushing against her cheeks, his wild eye boggling into hers.

'The **CRYPTOGOG** holds the secret.'

'What secret?' asked Mabel.

Leonard smiled. 'The final hiding-place of the DOOMSDAY BOOK!'

Mabel scratched her head.

'Where can I find the Cryptogog?'

Leonard looked glumly at the floor.

'Grand Zhool has the Cryptogog.'

He silenced another fit of the giggles with one of his long-fingered hands.

'But he can't open it.'

Mabel scratched her head. 'Open it?'

'Cryptogog is a special box. Very special,' hooted Leonard.

'Why doesn't he just smash it open?'

'Smashing the box will destroy the secret it contains.'

'So how do you open it?'

'Shhh!' said the librarian. 'Am reading.'

He put his long hands together and opened them as if reading an imaginary book.

Mabel reached for his arm.

'Please. I *need* to know how to open the Cryptogog!'

The librarian scowled at her.

'Shhh. Good bit. You leave, please.' He pretended to turn a page.

Carefully Mabel took the candle and started to climb down the empty bookshelf.

'Only the humble shall succeed,' murmured

Leonard, turning another imaginary page. 'Only the humble . . .'

Mabel felt sorry for the librarian. It seemed as though the years of solitude and the destruction of his beloved books had driven him **mad**. As she reached the bottom, she looked up at him one last time.

'Goodbye, Leonard,' she called.

The gibbon closed his imaginary book. His sad eye fixed on her and he spoke in the softest and quietest of voices.

'**The magic word, Mabel**. What's the magic word?'

'The magic word for what?'

Leonard jerked his head to one side and fixed her with his wild eye. Then, hooting angrily, he swung off into the gloom.

CHAPTER SIXTEEN
The Plan

'So,' explained Mabel Jones in the darkness of the alleyway that ran behind the **Grand Library**, 'all we need is to break into the **Grand Palace** and steal the Cryptogog.'

Omynus Hussh rubbed his doorknob with his good paw and smiled.

'Filchsome thievery? I knows just the loris for the job!'

He rubbed his head against Mabel and looked up at her with his saucery eyes.

'Then when I gots the Cryptothingummy, I'll slits the Grand Zhool's throat and rifle his pockets and steal his rings and we'll buy a pirate ship and –'

'We only need to get the Cryptogog, Omynus,' Mabel interrupted, frowning. Omynus meant well, but old habits die hard for a silent loris trained in

bloodthirsty piracy

since birth. 'I think we should all go.'

Jarvis brushed the hair from his eyes.

'We'll need some kind of **distraction**. Something or somebody good at causing a disruption . . .'

Everyone turned to stare at Speke.

'What's that, chaps?' he said, looking up from a notice on the wall. 'I'm afraid I was miles away.'

He pointed to the notice:

PORTRAIT ARTIST
WANTED
APPLY TO:
GOVVEL
AT THE GRAND PALACE

Clever, cunning Mabel Jones smiled. A plan had formed in her mind.

And, just in case it didn't at that same moment form in your mind, be quiet, for Mabel is about to explain . . .

'Speke, you can infiltrate the palace in the guise of a visiting portrait artist.'

Speke clapped his paws together in delight.

'Subterfuge! How jolly.' He paused. 'I think Carruthers should accompany me, though. I'll need someone to open the paints. They can be awfully tricky with webbed paws.'

Mabel nodded and continued. 'Then, while you two distract the Grand Zhool, me, Jarvis and Omynus will break in and **Steal the Cryptogog**!'

She looked at the otter.

'Are you sure you're happy to do this, Sir Timothy? It's very dangerous.'

Speke took a deep breath and his chest swelled with pride.

'For **ALBEMARLE**, I'll do it.'

Unnoticed by his friends, Speke's hand crept to his waistcoat pocket, where he kept his dear departed father's medal. 'And for Daddy,' he whispered, a tiny tear forming in his eye.

'I say,' said the muffled voice of Carruthers. 'Now you've formed your cunning plan, do you think you could unwedge me from this window?'

CHAPTER SEVENTEEN
Letters Home

For the attention of:

Sir Lockheed Beagle, Head of the Albemarle Top-secret Service

This just in from our Near Far Eastern division: a coded message from Agent Badger-Badger. Requires your urgent attention.

Springfeather

Dear Uncle,

We have finished Grandad's portrait and found a delightful frame. It is a great work of art and could surely hang in the Palace of the Grand Zhool. Sorry to hear about Grandma's face. Maybe she could have an operation to remove the tattoo if it truly is as rude as you describe. The judge will throw the book at her as it is her third prosecution for gross indecency this year. Surely she will be going to jail again. I guess you could keep her from view. Have you tried keeping her down the well?

Your nephew,

CARRUTHERS

Dearest Nanny Mimsy,
Our awfully important secret mission to steal that book I told you about is going rather well. Mother would be so proud. I remember her fondly joking, 'Your useless art will get you nowhere, Timothy,' as she filed my latest childish doodles carefully behind the dustbin.

But actually it seems my scribblings have come in rather handy. I have successfully applied to paint the Grand Zhool's portrait!

It will be the perfect distraction while my friends rifle through his palace in search of the Cryptogog. Hopefully we will find it before that bounder Von Klaar.

Anyway, better dash – I'm having my whiskers trimmed in preparation for tomorrow's exciting spy work.

All my love,
Timmy
x x x x x x x x x

PS Have you seen Algernon Teddy? He wasn't in my suitcase. I'm afraid I'm not sleeping well without him.

CHAPTER EIGHTEEN

The Beggar

ICE CREAM! ICE CREAM! WHO WILL BUY MY WONDERFUL ICE CREAM?

Hello.

I'VE GOT STRAWBERRY . . .

It's me.

RASPBERRY . . .

The narrator!

TUTTI-FRUTTI . . .

Don't you recognize me?

PICKLED ONION . . .

I am in disguise. As an ice-cream seller!

ALL MADE WITH FRESH MILK, HAND-SQUEEZED FRESH FROM THE SKUNK'S TEAT!

Quick! Duck behind my trolley.

Dawn is breaking and we are approaching our desired position in the busy market that fills the **Great Square**.

Push through the crowds.

So.

Many.

Pilgrims.

Though the day has only just dawned, the **Great Square** has been turned over to the market traders and merchants, and the city is awake and looking for bargains.

It is often said that you can buy **anything** from the market at **Otom**.

Here an old whaler from the **FROZEN NORTH** sells the furs from a colony of **hand-clubbed seals**.

'I throws in a **narwhal tusk** if ye buys more than a dozen.'

Behind him, the narwhal peers unhappily from a rusty tin bath full of grimy water.

A mysterious ibis from the far-away deserts of *The Unknown* sells shiny brooches in the shape of **large scarab beetles**. Such baubles are popular among wealthy Otomites, but beware – that is no ordinary trinket!

The beetle is actually **alive** and trained to play dead until you fall asleep, when it will go through your pockets and run back to the merchant with as much of your spare change as it can carry.

Yes, anything you could possibly want: **steamed mackerel** from the *Cold Grey Sea*, exotic **spiced tobacco** from the Near Far East, or soft and creamy **lizard cheese** from the coastal forests of the **NOO WORLD**.

Anything you could possibly want . . .

Or steal.

For the market is home to the **honest** and the **dishonest** alike. The rich man, the poor man, the tinker, the thief and the beggar.

And the living statue. Although don't give that one any money – he actually died last week and no one's noticed yet. That's not performance art. That's **rigor mortis.**

Mabel Jones scratched her bum. The heavy monk's robes she was wearing to conceal her hooman features were made of a particularly itchy fabric. She cautiously lifted the hood a little and looked around.

'Where is he?' she hissed at the monk next to her.

Jarvis peered back at her from beneath his own hood.

'I don't know. He's been gone a while. Maybe he's been caught!'

'Omynus is never caught! Besides, he's only supposed to be looking for a secret way into the palace.' Mabel frowned. 'I hope he's not stealing anything.'

'I's not been stealing nothing,' said a sulky voice from behind them.

Mabel turned round.

'Hello, Omynus.' She went to scratch his head, but the loris pulled away.

'I's found a ways in but it's too **dangerous-deadly-difficult** for you,' he said, folding his skinny arms.

'I'm sorry, Omynus,' said Mabel. 'I'm sure you weren't stealing. Show us the way in you've found.'

As she spoke, Mabel sidestepped to avoid a gopher in a conical hat who was pushing through the crowd towards the **cute and fluffy chick stall**.

He glared at her.

'Mind where you tread!'

Mabel turned momentarily to apologize, forgetting that her face was still partly exposed.

The gopher's eyes narrowed.

'You! What kind of creature are you?'

Mabel pulled her robes closer to her face.

'Just a humble **bald-faced monkey**, Your Worship.'

The gopher scowled and returned to browsing

cute and fluffy chicks. 'I'll take a punnet of twelve,' he snapped to the merchant. 'And make sure they're good and plump.'

Mabel turned back to Jarvis and Omynus.

'Come on,' she said. 'It's too dangerous here.'

But, as she turned to go, Mabel felt a hand tugging at her robe.

'Any money for a poor sailor who's got no eyes?'

'I'm afraid I haven't got any money,' replied Mabel, looking nervously back towards the gopher.

The beggar tugged on her robe again, delving his paw deep into her pocket.

'Any money for a poor sailor who's got no legs?'

There were three guardsmen with the gopher now. They were all looking at her **suspiciously**.

'Please! I have to go!'

Mabel pulled at her robe, but still the creature held on.

'Any money for a poor sailor who's got no hope?'

Mabel Jones finally looked down upon her unfortunate assailant. There, sitting in the gutter, small face peering from a bundle of filthy rags, was a **guinea pig.**

There was something strangely familiar about this beggar, though. Something about the eyes that bulged out from behind his round sunglasses . . .

The beggar smiled a toothy smile. Then he bellowed:

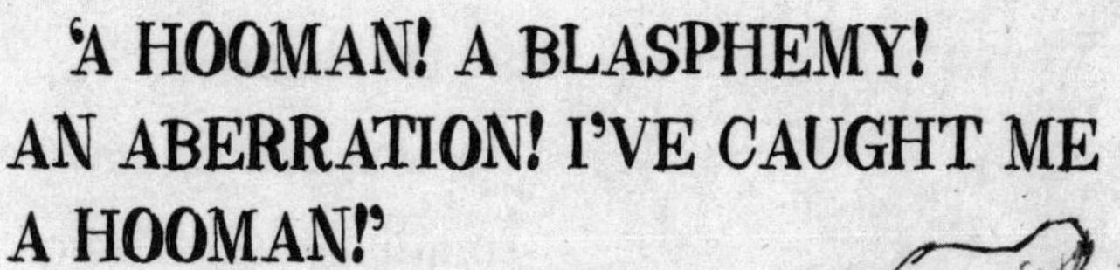

'A HOOMAN! A BLASPHEMY! AN ABERRATION! I'VE CAUGHT ME A HOOMAN!'

The gopher whirled round.

'I knew it! Seize that cloaked creature!'

'Quick, run!' yelled Mabel, yanking herself free.

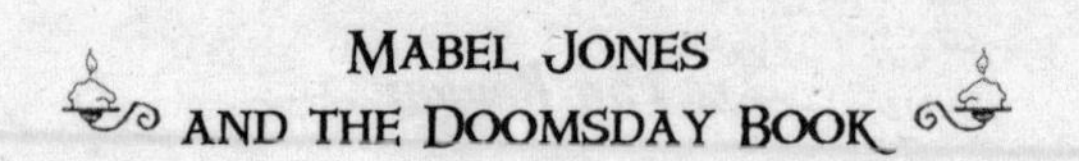

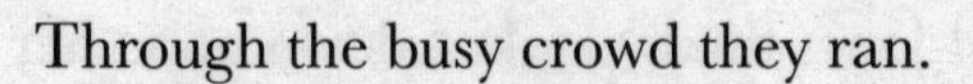

Through the busy crowd they ran.

Ignoring the shouts of startled market-goers, Mabel, Jarvis and Omynus ducked and weaved through the stalls and dashed into a narrow, dark alleyway that led away from the square.

A dead end!

Mabel looked back from the shadows.

A wolf soldier was standing at the end of the alleyway.

He hadn't seen them yet, but if he just turned his head a fraction . . .

'Look!' whispered Jarvis. 'Steps!'

Steps that led down into the darkness.

The wolf soldier was joined by another. Muskets drawn, they began to edge cautiously into the alley.

Quickly the three friends scampered down the steps. They led to a rusting metal grate that blocked the entrance to a dark tunnel.

Another dead end!

Jarvis grabbed the grate and shook it. It wouldn't budge.

'We're done for!'

'Spread out and search everywhere,' said the wolf from the top of the steps. 'The **blasphemy** ran this way. It must be around here somewhere . . .'

The wolf took a sausage from behind his ear and munched on it as the other soldiers dispersed. Mopping his brow with a handkerchief, he peered down the steps into the darkness.

'Probably nothing down there . . .' His stomach rumbled. 'Better get back to the barracks for lunch.'

Mabel sighed with relief. The soldier was leaving! Maybe there was still time to get into the palace before Speke and Carruthers set off their **distraction**.

But Mabel Jones had sighed too soon.

For suddenly the wolf dropped his sausage. It teetered at the top for a moment and then, to Mabel's horror, began bouncing down the steps towards them.

Closer it bounced . . .

Closer . . .

And closer . . .

Before finally coming to a standstill at Mabel's feet.

She tried to shuffle further back into the shadows, but there was nowhere left to shuffle.

And now the wolf was cautiously padding down the steps.

Closer he came . . .

Closer . . .

And closer . . .

'Where is that bloomin' sausage?'

Mabel held her breath. In mere moments the wolf would be able to see them. She gripped her cutlass and –

A tiny scruffy rat face appeared through a hole in the grate right next to Mabel's head.

'You are in **EXTREME DANGER**!' it whispered.

Mabel blinked in agreement, too afraid to move or speak.

The rat's face disappeared back into the darkness and a small door concealed in the grate slid open noiselessly – almost as though it had been **well oiled** in preparation for an occasion such as this.

Quickly Mabel, Omynus and Jarvis stepped into the dark tunnel. The door slid silently closed behind them.

'This way,' hissed the rat, wrapping a dark raincoat round himself. He shambled further into the gloom.

The friends followed the creature, feeling their way deeper underground. They were safe again – but for how long?

What were these mysterious tunnels?

And **who** was their mysterious guide?

CHAPTER NINETEEN
Their Mysterious Guide

Mabel could barely see the tiny rat as he shambled down the dark, damp and dripping tunnel. He was a curious creature, hunched over and limping slightly. The rat paused, leaning on an old cotton bud for support, then spasmed into a dry and scrapey coughing fit.

Mabel squatted down beside him. Beneath the dirty coat that dragged along the floor, Mabel could see bald patches in his fur. His eyes were caked with **crusty grime**.

'Are you OK?'

The rat coughed again.

'It's just **sewer fever**. I've got the filthy dampness in my lungs and there's no cure apart from fresh air and clean underpants.'

Jarvis peered into the gloom, his nose wrinkling.

'This is a sewer?'

The rat nodded. 'Indeed. These tunnels belong to the sewers of an ancient city built and

abandoned before the founding of **Otom**. A hooman city!'

He paused and fumbled inside his pocket. Then there was the sound of a striking match, and a fuse hanging from the wall of the tunnel caught fire with a bright flame that burnt upward to a dim lamp hanging on the side of the tunnel. Another fuse sparked and burnt along the length of the tunnel to another lamp. Then another fuse was lit. Then another and another until the long tunnel was illuminated in a **flickering glow**.

The brick-lined tunnel sloped gently downward into the gloom.

A small trickle of dirty water ran between their feet and soaked into Mabel's slippers. And all along the tunnel's length were openings to other tunnels: some smaller, some larger and some as huge as vaulted chambers.

All **gloomy.**

All **cold.**

All **damp.**

And all **very,**

VERY

smelly.

'Where are you taking us?' asked Mabel.

The rat smiled grimly.

'You'll see.'

They turned sharply into a side tunnel, then sharply once more into a smaller tunnel that led to a tight spiral staircase leading down. The rat turned to Mabel and held out a trembling paw.

'Would you be so kind? My bones are weakened from the darkness, and the stairs are slippery with the slime of ages.'

'Of course,' said Mabel, taking the rat by the paw as they carefully descended the staircase. 'I'm Mabel, by the way. Mabel Jones.'

The rat looked up at her with a tired smile.

'May St Statham bless your kindness, Mabel Jones.'

'And this is Jarvis and Omynus Hussh.'

The rat nodded to them politely.

'You are all welcome,' he said, gesturing through a huge arched opening. 'Please, my home is this way.'

The three friends **gasped**.

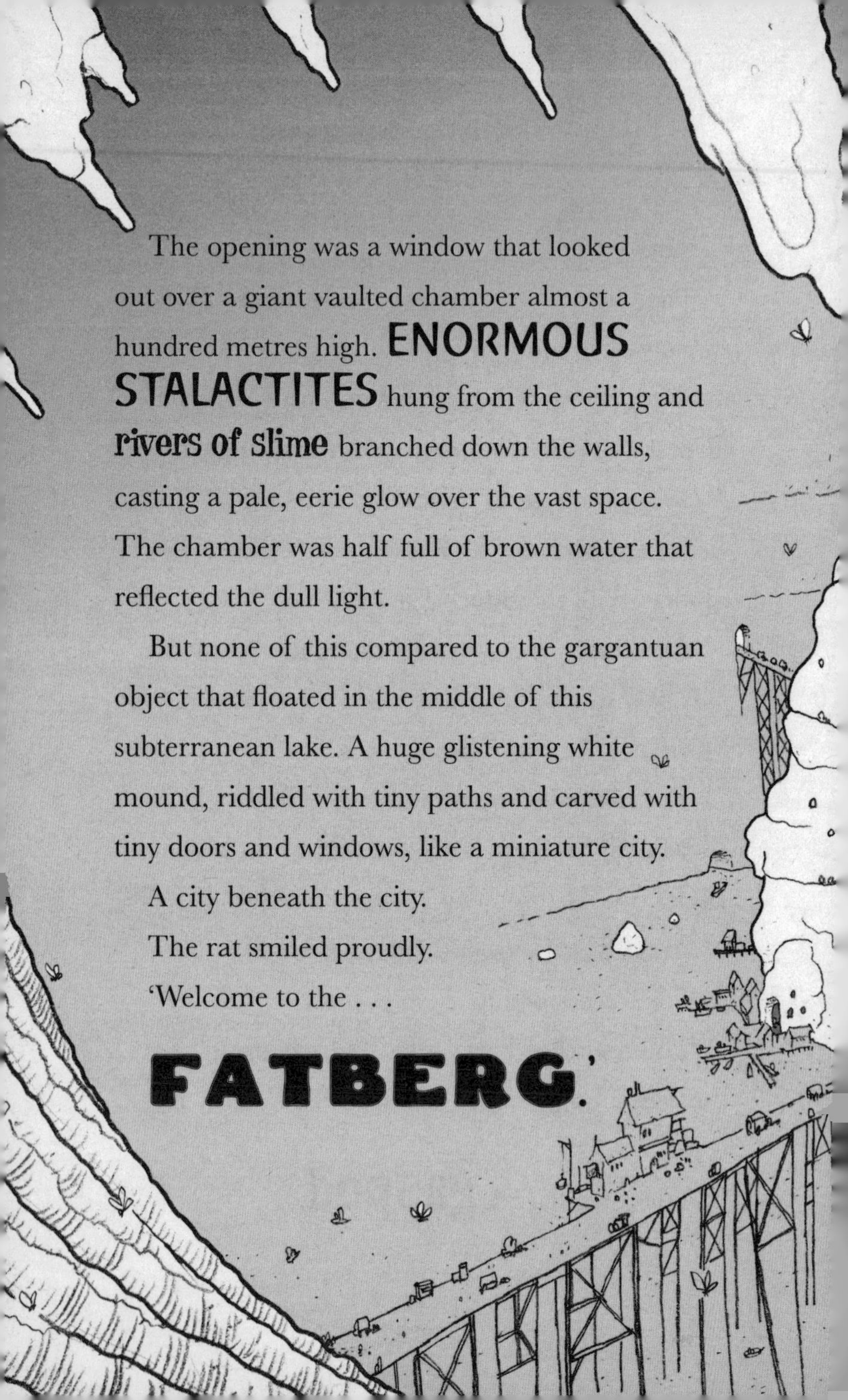

The opening was a window that looked out over a giant vaulted chamber almost a hundred metres high. **ENORMOUS STALACTITES** hung from the ceiling and **rivers of slime** branched down the walls, casting a pale, eerie glow over the vast space. The chamber was half full of brown water that reflected the dull light.

But none of this compared to the gargantuan object that floated in the middle of this subterranean lake. A huge glistening white mound, riddled with tiny paths and carved with tiny doors and windows, like a miniature city.

A city beneath the city.

The rat smiled proudly.

'Welcome to the . . .

FATBERG.'

CHAPTER TWENTY
The Afterlife of a Bacon Sandwich

We are in your own time now, reader. No longer in the footure but in your doomed hooman age, in a hustling and bustling, thriving city. You may recognize the grand buildings, the proud bridges and vainglorious monuments. Hold them in your mind. For soon they will be derelict, fallen or crumbled.

Time is running out and we must be quick – I for one do not wish to be present when ***The End*** comes. But it is not ***The End*** in which we are interested. Not quite yet. We are interested in a **beginning**.

The beginning of the FATBERG.

Follow me down an unusual path that begins with the eating of a bacon sandwich and the subsequent washing-up of a used frying-pan.

The rendered fat from that bacon is swept down the plughole by a jet of clean water and a liberal squeeze of washing-up liquid. Through the pipes of the kitchen it winds until it joins the main drain, where the warm liquid fat meets the rest of the sandwich – albeit **chewed**, **digested** and **compacted**.

Its component parts reunited, our former

bacon sandwich continues its journey to the sewer, where it joins the similarly **filthy** remnants of hooman life that your species gaily flushes from sight.

There it separates again, the bacon fat cooling and solidifying, settling against the wall of the tunnels in **glistening globules** of coagulated lard, bound together with the other insoluble debris of hooman life. The wet wipes, the flushed toys, the **hooman hair** . . .

Eventually it breaks free of its sticky moorings and travels on, deeper into the sewer, until it meets other floating masses of congealed fat, which it joins.

And so it continues, day after day, until one day it is too big to move any further.

And there it remains. Trapped.

A floating berg of solid fat.

Growing. And **growing**.

And **growing**.

A white, sweating, monstrous form lurking beneath the city.

Until, years from your time, deep, deep into the footure, it is **found.**

Found by the very rat now sitting with Mabel, Jarvis and Omynus Hussh in a round chamber hollowed into the centre of the

FATBERG.

The rat wrapped his raincoat round his hunched and mangy body. Wiping his dripping nose on the back of a paw, he began to talk . . .

'My name is **Findus**, and this is my story.'

CHAPTER TWENTY-ONE
Findus

'He hates us.'

Findus shivered and pulled his coat closer still.

'The Grand Zhool hates me and every one of my family.'

Mabel looked around. She hadn't seen any other rats in the **FATBERG**. Maybe they'd popped out for some shopping or something.

'But why?' asked Jarvis.

'He hates us because he fears us. And he fears us because he thinks we are dirty. He thinks rats are the second dirtiest species of all time. And he **hates** dirt.' Findus smiled sadly. 'But we weren't dirty before he banished us to the ancient stinking sewers.'

Jarvis frowned.

'Why did he banish you?'

Findus frowned thoughtfully.

'Nobody knows for sure. But it was ten years ago, just after that outbreak of the **DEADLY PLAGUE**.'

He smiled at his new friends and continued. 'Anyway, what we *do* know is that there is only one species he hates and fears more than rats. The species that built this stinking sewer, the **dirtiest** species to have ever lived . . .'

Mabel looked at Jarvis.

Jarvis looked at her.

'Hoomans!' they said together.

The rat nodded.

'That's right, comrades.'

He stood, clenching his tiny paw.

'But soon the foul winds of change will blow out of the sewers and through the streets of **Otom**. No longer will my family be confined underground. Tomorrow, on the **FESTIVAL OF ST STATHAM**, we will rise up, our courage against his army. The fight will be tough. Many rats will fall in the streets of **Otom**, but in the end we will be free!'

Findus sat down again.

'I just hopc there's enough of us.'

Mabel looked around. Now she thought about it, she hadn't seen any other rats at all since she'd entered the sewers. The odds didn't look good, so she coughed politely and changed the subject.

'We're trying to get into the **Grand Palace**. To steal something from the Grand Zhool.'

Findus placed his little paw on Mabel's hand.

'These tunnels spread beneath the whole city. To the novice they are an **impenetrable labyrinth**, but I know the exact one you need. It climbs upward into the chambers of the Grand Zhool himself.'

He paused for dramatic effect.

'You need to climb the **Filthpipe**!'

CHAPTER TWENTY-TWO

The Filthpipe

Mabel looked at the dark hole in front of her. It was barely wide enough for her to squeeze into. The smell was almost overpowering.

I can't do it . . .

She looked over at Findus.

'Have you ever climbed it?'

Findus scratched his scabby belly, sending flakes of dried skin floating down into the filthy water that trickled past their feet. He screwed his little nose up.

'Never,' he said. 'Only the dirtiest species can brave the **Filthpipe**.'

Mabel grimaced.

I really can't do it . . .

Then she thought of her mum and dad, and Maggie, her little sister. Sometime – sometime soon for them perhaps – a mystery event would wipe out all the hoomans.

She needed to find out what that event was. Then maybe, just maybe, she would be able to stop it. But to do that she needed to find the **DOOMSDAY BOOK**.

'My name is Mabel Jones and I'm not scared of anything.'

And, with those words, she gripped the rim of the hole and began to haul herself upward.

CHAPTER TWENTY-THREE
A Cunning Distraction

The Grand Zhool pressed his snout into the *luxurious* fur collar of his luxurious fur coat and stretched his stubby legs. Then he repositioned himself slightly on his **magnificent gilded throne** and slowly opened his colossal jaws.

Reaching into a small velvet bag, Govvel pulled out a fluffy yellow chick and placed it carefully in the Grand Zhool's mouth, which slowly closed with a small, soft cracking noise.

Sir Timothy Speke coughed politely. He was looking at the Zhool with one eye closed, framing him between his small webbed paws.

'If you'd just hold still a moment, Your Grace. I'm trying to capture your, erm . . . regal stateliness before the sun sets.'

He looked nervously out of the window.

Govvel sneered.

'And make sure you do. The first artist we hired made it look like he was Smiling.'

'I say, how jolly!'

The gopher shook his head.

'It was the last portrait he ever painted.'

Speke giggled nervously and rubbed out the smile he had drawn. Then he knelt down behind his small cart of paints, saying, 'I'll just fetch some crimson. For the, er, gums.'

He lowered his voice to a whisper. 'Carruthers? Carruthers? Are you receiving me?'

A secret panel in the cart slid open and a very squashed-looking badger peered out.

'Of course I am,' he hissed back. 'I'm right here, remember?'

'I'm scared, Carruthers,' whispered Speke. 'It's the fur coat, you know. Fur's always difficult and every time I look at it, it seems to have moved slightly!'

'Nonsense, Timothy. I believe in you. You are the finest artist in all of **CRUMBRIDGE**, if not the whole of **ALBEMARLE**.'

'I say! Thanks, old boy. You know what? I do feel a bit better now.'

Carruthers's paw held out a tube of red paint.

'It's only horses you're terrible at, Timothy. Your portrait of SIR FREDERICK GALLOPS was a real stinker. It looked like his legs were on back to front.'

'Now, Carruthers, that's jolly unfair.'

'Steady yourself, Timothy. All we have to do is cause a **distraction**. Our timed

smoke grenade

will do that when we have safely left the palace. Then Mabel and the others will do the thievery.'

'Yes, they are rather good at that sort of thing, aren't they?'

Speke looked around to check he wasn't being

overheard. Govvel was feeding the Grand Zhool another chick.

'Do you have the **distraction** ready?' he whispered.

There was the sound of a portly badger repositioning himself within a confined space, and a paw poked out of the hatch holding a small smoke bomb.

'Ripping!' squeaked Speke, taking it from him. 'Just like the jolly japes we got up to at **ST CRISPIN'S SCHOOL FOR THE EXCEEDINGLY RICH**.'

Carruthers pressed an angry eye to the hatch.

'Shush, Timothy! The smoke bomb is set to go off in one hour from now, when we are safely back aboard the *Sunbeam*. So, whatever you do, don't remove the safety pin or the **distraction** will go off almost immediately.'

'You mean this one?' said Speke, holding out the removed safety pin towards the hatch.

BOOM!

CHAPTER TWENTY-FOUR

A Dirty Job

Make haste! The plushly carpeted corridors of the Grand Zhool's palace may dampen the sound of our running footsteps, but I fear we will still be heard. Our plans to take up a stealthy position ready to document the next chapter of Carruthers and Speke's mission have taken a turn for the worse.

A **Situation** has occurred.

An **EMERGENCY**!

Curse these never-ending corridors, these unlabelled doors, these plaster busts of important dignitaries that stare expressionlessly as we scamper past!

Faster!

Throw caution to the wind, for time is running out.

This way!

No, that way!

A PLAGUE ON THIS PIOUS PALACE OF PRINCELY POMP!

We *must* find it.

We must –

Aha!

We *have* found it!

There! The door marked **TOILET**.

Open it! But take care no one is inside.

Me? No, you look first!

Empty?

Phew.

Incredible place, isn't it? I'll be checking your pockets later, so don't feel tempted to prise one of those **SAPPHIRES** from the toilet seat. We must leave no evidence of ever having been here. For this toilet belongs to no ordinary person.

You can tell by the luxurious stoat-skin bottom-wiper.

Feel it.

Soft and

strong and

biodegradable!

Now put the stoat back in his cage. He has the most horrid of jobs and the unfortunate creature needs his rest.

But, yes, as you must by now have guessed, this is the personal en-suite bathroom of the Grand Zhool himself!

Anyway, back to the important matter in hand.

You wait here while I use the cubicle.

I beg your pardon? You'd rather I closed the door?

Well, if I must but –

WHAT WAS THAT? Disaster!

I fear that my business will forever remain undone!

Quickly, reader, conceal yourself.

There is a **grunting** . . .

a **groaning** . . .

a **moaning** . . .

It's coming from deep within this toilet bowl.

What else can it be but some foul creature of the underworld rising to the surface in search of a victim? What is this beast? This stinking, sewer-dwelling **monstrosity** . . .

It's . . .

Grasping fingers grip the rim of the toilet.

It's . . .

A face emerges, hair plastered to its head with **fetid stinkwater**.

It's . . .

A body heaves itself out and collapses in a breathless heap upon the floor, then looks up and absent-mindedly picks its nose.

IT'S MABEL JONES!

Yes, sodden, stinking Mabel Jones! She has braved the **Filthpipe**!

Another creature hauls itself free of the toilet. Jarvis. Similarly sodden and stinking.

Now a third. A silence falls upon the room as Omynus Hussh creeps from the bowl.

Stinking, filth-covered Mabel Jones wiped her filthy face on her filthy pyjamas and looked around the bathroom. 'We've got to find the Cryptogog,' she whispered.

Very, very slowly she pushed open the door to the Grand Zhool's chambers.

A strange thick smoke cloaked the room and chairs were overturned as though someone had recently let off a smoke bomb and a struggle had taken place.

'Speke and Carruthers's **distraction**!' Mabel whispered to Jarvis.

Jarvis smiled. 'Looks like their plan worked!'

Mabel nodded. 'But it's gone off a bit early.'

'So now what?'

'Now we search for the Cryptogog. Leonard said it's a special box, but we don't know what it looks like. We need to split up and –'

Omynus Hussh coughed politely.

'Is this it?'

He held out a small iron box with the word **CRYPTOGOG** written on the top.

Mabel Jones gawped.

'How did you do that?!'

Omynus grinned.

'I is the bestest thief ever,' he said, his furry face blushing slightly.

CHAPTER TWENTY-FIVE

Cracking the Cryptogog

The stars shine over the docks of **Otom**; their soft, sparkly light catches on the rolling tide and rides to the shore upon the gentle lapping waves. From the city comes the chime of the cathedral bells, which travels upon the warm and briny winds like –

You get the picture.

Basically it is fifteen minutes to midnight on the night before the **FESTIVAL OF ST STATHAM**.

In the cabin of the **Sunbeam**, Mabel, Jarvis

and Omynus were examining the Cryptogog.

Jarvis turned the box round in his hands.

'Maybe we should wait for Speke and Carruthers. They should have been back by now. I wonder where they've got to?'

Mabel frowned. 'Perhaps something went wrong with the **distraction**.'

Jarvis looked at her over the box. 'You don't think they've been **captured**, do you?'

'Don't worry, Jarvis. I'm sure they'll turn up soon,' said Mabel. 'Knowing Speke, they probably stopped off for tea and crumpets.'

Jarvis squinted at the box in his hands.

'Here . . . At first it seems like there's no opening at all. No crack or anything. But look: five tiny hatches!'

Mabel peered closely. Sure enough, on one end of the box there was a tiny circular hatch.

She carefully tried to open it.

Nothing.

'"Only the humble shall succeed",' she muttered, remembering the words of Leonard the librarian. '"The magic word, Mabel. What's the magic word?"'

She looked at Jarvis.

'Do you know any magic words?'

'Alakazam?'

Nothing.

'Abracadabra!'

Nothing.

Omynus Hussh looked at the box. The fingers of his good hand danced nimbly across its iron surface, probing for some sort of weakness or a hidden switch.

'Even my lovely loris fingers can't unpicks this,' he said in disgust.

Jarvis stood up and stretched.

'This could take a bit of time. Maybe we should have a snack?' he said, reaching for a tin of ship's biscuits.

'There's no time for snacks,' Mabel snapped. 'We need to find the **DOOMSDAY BOOK**. The fate of the hooman race depends upon it. So does Pelf's freedom and the safety of **ALBEMARLE**. We **MUST** get to it before Von Klaar!'

Her stomach rumbled.

'Pass the biscuits.'

Jarvis pushed the tin towards Mabel, but as she paused to choose between a plain or a **weevil** biscuit he snatched it away again. 'What's the magic word?'

Mabel gasped!

The answer had just tumbled from his mouth! 'Please! **"Please"** is the magic word!'

She picked up the box and spoke.

'Please open, Cryptogog!'

And with that humble request there came a tiny scraping noise from within the box. Slowly the circular hatch rotated. A bit to the left. Then to the right. Then back to the left.

And then . . .

With a loud click, and for the first time since it had been sealed . . .

THE CRYPTOGOG OPENED!

Mabel and Jarvis looked at the circular hole.

A piece of sawdust fell out.

Then some more.

Then a wizened, wrinkled head emerged.

THE HEAD OF AN ANCIENT TORTOISE!

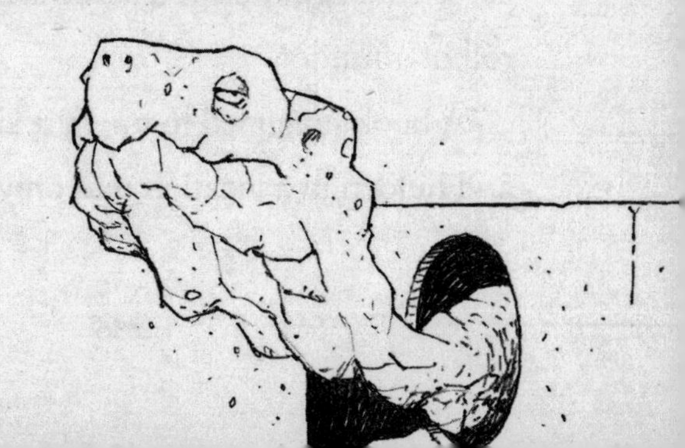

It blinked. Then coughed. Then spoke in a quiet rasping voice.

'I am the Cryptogog . . .'

It slowly moved its head to look at Mabel. Then slowly it looked at Jarvis.

'Two hooman snuglets,' it croaked, smiling.

Mabel gently placed the tortoise and its box on the deck.

The Cryptogog nodded his head slowly in thanks.

'You wish to learn of the location of the
DOOMSDAY BOOK.'

He paused as, far out to sea, lightning danced across the sky, followed some seconds after by a roll of thunder.

'A book smuggled to me by a kind junior librarian and hidden in a location that only I know!'

Mabel and Jarvis nodded dumbly.

The tortoise continued.

'For ten long years I have remained in **hibernation**, awaiting the arrival of one so humble as to speak the magic word.'

He peered at them through crusty eyes.

'For only the humble can be trusted with the powerful secrets contained within the DOOMSDAY BOOK.'

He coughed again.

'And now I can finally share my secret. A secret kept for ten long years.'

The Cryptogog blinked. A look of worry crossed his face.

'I'm not sure I can remember, though. For I am old. A hundred years old.'

'You *must* remember!' pleaded Mabel.

The tortoise smiled.

'Ah yes. That's it. I'll start again. For ten long years I have remained in hibernation . . .'

He paused to cough some more.

Jarvis sighed. 'We've done this bit. Could you skip to the location of the DOOMSDAY BOOK?'

The tortoise frowned.

'If you wish. For I have kept this secret for ten long years and I am a hundred years old . . .'

He paused for dramatic effect.

'The DOOMSDAY BOOK is hidden in the **Grand Cathedral of Otom**. I used to be the organist, you see.'

The Cryptogog coughed another dry cough.

'I fear my life is almost over. For I am a hundred years old and Death creeps nearer with every passing moment and now the secret needs to be spoken. Where was I? Ah yes . . . I have been in hibernation for ten long years. The DOOMSDAY BOOK is hidden in . . .'

He choked a little.

'The DOOMSDAY BOOK will be revealed when . . .'

Then, with a slight gurgle, the Cryptogog slowly closed his eyes.

Mabel swallowed.

She looked at Jarvis.

'I think he's . . .

I think he's

dead.'

But he wasn't.

With a gasp, the Cryptogog's eyes opened wide with fear.

'May St Statham have mercy on my soul! Death is upon me and my secret has not yet been told – for I have been alive for one hundred years and I have kept my secret for the last ten of those. The secret is . . .'

He coughed again. His eyes began to close.

'The secret is . . .'

Another cough.

'The secret is . . .'

'What?' exclaimed Mabel and Jarvis in unison.

'CABBAGE.'

And, with that final word, the Cryptogog's eyes rolled backwards and his head lolled limply from the iron box.

Mabel swallowed again.

'I think he's . . . dead.'

And this time he was.

CHAPTER TWENTY-SIX
The Mummified Remains of St Statham

Close your eyes in silent prayer, press your hands together in thankfulness and cast the ashes of your dead gerbil Gavin into the warm wind that blows in from the *Calm Blue Sea*. For midnight has struck! The **FESTIVAL OF ST STATHAM** has begun!

Through the perfectly clean and tidy streets of **Otom** runs a never-ending stream of pilgrims, their procession lit by a thousand burning torches.

All heading to the same place.

The magnificent . . .

The gargantuan . . .

The incredible . . .

Grand Cathedral of Otom!

We have seen it before. Its vast spire casts a long shadow over the city and over our story. At night it is even more impressive. Its gilded dome, reflecting the moonlight, shines like a **beacon**.

A beacon that calls the followers of St Statham from hundreds, nay, thousands of miles away.

Inside the cathedral, three shadowy figures push through the crowds high up in the gallery. The only three figures not awaiting the arrival of the Grand Zhool on this, the most holy of days. These figures have a different mission.

For somewhere inside this cathedral is hidden a book.

THE DOOMSDAY BOOK!

And if Mabel Jones and her companions can find this book, then maybe, just maybe, the end of the hooman species can be averted, their friend Pelf freed and war between **ALBEMARLE** and **Alsatia** prevented.

The three friends gather beside the large organ. Its golden pipes snake and twist upward into the vaulted ceiling.

Jarvis scratched his head. 'The Cryptogog said he used to be the organist. Maybe we should start by looking here.'

Omynus Hussh, an expert finder-outer of hidden secrets, probed the niches of the ancient organ with the long and nimble fingers of his good hand.

'If it's here, it's hidden good and sneaksome, snuglets,' he muttered.

But, while her friends searched, Mabel's mind was on other matters.

Where are Speke and Carruthers?
Why didn't they return
to the *Sunbeam*?

Nothing had been seen of them since they had caused their **distraction**.

What if they've been caught?

Mabel thrust the thought to the back of her mind. They had to find the DOOMSDAY BOOK before Von Klaar got there first. After that, there would be time to find Speke and Carruthers.

Suddenly the chatter of the congregation hushed to a fearful silence. The moon had reached its zenith, and its light fell through the stained-glass window and shone a rainbow of light upon the High Altar, where a large hippopotamus stood, clad in a fur coat.

THE GRAND ZHOOL!

The Grand Zhool slowly turned from the altar to face the silent crowd, raising his fat hand in a solemn gesture of welcome.

'Friends . . .'

His deep voice, amplified by the dome, echoed about the cathedral as though it was the voice of St Statham himself.

Mabel's eyes scanned the crowd. Maybe Speke and Carruthers were in the cathedral somewhere. It seemed that everyone in **Otom** was here.

The Grand Zhool smiled.

'Fellow followers of St Statham, founder of the great city of **Otom**, we are here today to celebrate his memory.'

He paused. Not a creature moved.

'But on this most holy day a sordid, despicable filth gathers in our beautiful city. A **toxic slime** from the distant shores of a far-off land.'

The crowd stirred nervously. The Grand Zhool pressed his fat hands together and closed his wrinkle-lidded eyes.

'This **toxic slime** has grown into an **evil canker** within these city walls. A growth that, if left unchecked, will spread like the **wicked warts of sin** across our beautiful city. Yes, there are those among us who wish evil upon **Otom**, those of us who wish evil upon the Grand

Zhool himself and thus upon the sacred memory of St Statham.'

Jarvis looked up from the organ.

'What was the last thing the Cryptogog said again?' he asked Mabel.

'Shh! I'm listening.'

Jarvis tugged her pyjama sleeve.

'Mabel?'

'He said "CABBAGE". Maybe he was hungry . . .'

Mabel trailed off. Something had caught her eye.

Far below, the unmistakable conical hat of Govvel was moving slowly down the aisle. A troop of soldiers followed at his heels.

And behind them?

The bound and blindfolded forms of Sir Timothy Speke and Carruthers Badger-Badger!

THEY *HAD* BEEN CAPTURED!

The sinister procession stopped beneath the large dome of the cathedral as the Grand Zhool continued to speak, his jowls flapping with rage.

'Yes, an evil that must be rooted out like a rotten tooth. For last night an attempt was made on the life of the Grand Zhool by agents of a foreign power!'

The crowd gasped.

The Grand Zhool pointed a podgy finger at Speke and Carruthers.

'**The Fur Coat of Righteousness** will decide their fate!'

Mabel gasped. She'd seen what the Fur Coat of Righteousness could do. Speke and Carruthers had no chance.

THERE WAS NOT A MOMENT TO LOSE!

'My name is Mabel Jones and I'm not scared of anything!'

And, with that cry, brave, foolish Mabel Jones leapt from the balcony on to a hanging tapestry that, unlike in almost every movie she had ever seen and every book she had ever read, immediately tore free of its supporting hooks, sending her falling to the ground below, her skull striking **hard** against the cold stone floor of the cathedral.

Well, that's what *would* have happened, had not a bear on a pilgrimage from the **BALTIC MOUNTAINS** cushioned her fall with his soft and ample pre-hibernation coat.

Apologizing, Mabel Jones stood up.

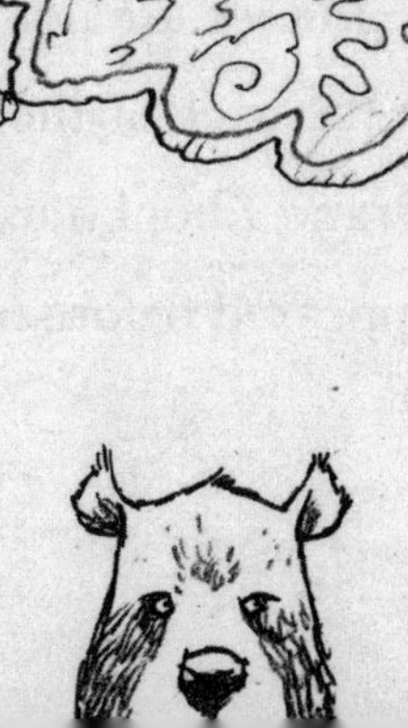

Then she looked around.

The whole congregation was staring at her.

The wet-lipped gopher was staring.

The Grand Zhool was staring.

In fact, the only person not looking at her was Jarvis, who hadn't even noticed her jump to the rescue of their friends. His mind was elsewhere and, if we were near enough to hear (which we are not, but if we were), then we would have heard him mutter to himself:

'CABBAGE?'

There was something strange about that word. Something about the letters . . .

And, if we were near enough to see (which we are not, but if we were), we would see him scratch his chin and look at the organ keyboard thoughtfully.

But we are not there. We are here. Concealed at the back of the congregation. Watching as the Grand Zhool stares at the nightmare that has appeared before him.

His face wore a look of pure revulsion.

'A hooman!'

His lips curled back, revealing his huge bone-white tombstone teeth.

'SEIZE THE ABOMINATION!'

All around the cathedral, the Grand Zhool's Personal Guard drew their swords and advanced on Mabel Jones.

Surrounded on all sides, she pulled the cutlass from her belt and cut the bonds that held her friends.

'I say, we're free!' cried Speke.

He removed his blindfold and surveyed the scene.

'Oh!'

'Don't despair,' shouted Carruthers gruffly. 'These halfwits haven't reckoned with the genius gadgetry of the **ALBEMARLE TOP-SECRET SERVICE!**'

Carruthers straightened his arm and pressed a cufflink with his paw.

Somewhere within his jacket, microscopic clockwork machinery released a spring, and from his shirt sleeve emerged a . . .

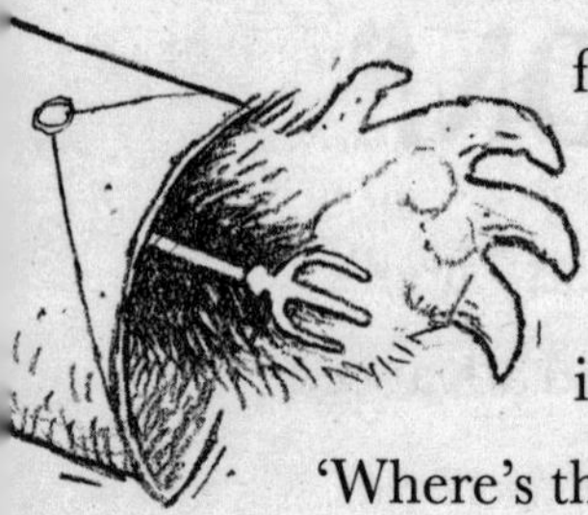

crumpet fork?

He glared at the toasting implement in fury.

'Where's the **CONCEALED BLUNDERBUSS**?' He turned to look at Speke. 'Timothy, you *didn't*?'

Speke twiddled his thumbs nervously.

'Well, I asked the boffins back in Crumbridge to make some small improvements,' he explained, pulling a crumpet from a secret compartment in his shoe heel. 'In case we found ourselves in need of an Emergency Tea.'

The Grand Zhool stepped forward through the ring of soldiers.

'**ENOUGH!**' he roared. 'Their time has come!'

His coat started to **move.**

Bright eyes blinked from within the soft shampooed fur.

Claws were **extended.**

The weasels were waking!

The cathedral fell into a hushed and horrified silence, and if someone had happened to have had a pin and accidentally dropped it then you probably would've heard it. Unless they dropped it on to a carpet or something like that.

Then a tuneless wailing filled the air. A long honking groan that built until it echoed all around the vast cathedral.

It was the drone of the ancient pipe organ. The same organ once played by the former organist of the **Grand Cathedral of Otom**, the Cryptogog!

And those of you blessed with the pitch-perfect ears of a particularly pitch-perfect pipistrelle will be able to identify the note played.

The same letter being silently mouthed, high above the action, by the concentrating Jarvis.

'**Middle C**,' he says to himself, his eyes fixed on the keyboard.

Then Jarvis plays an **A** and the drone changes.

Then a **B**, then another **B**.

Then the **A** again.

Then **G**.

And finally an **E**.

The word 'CABBAGE' spelt out in musical notes!

As the last note died away, it was replaced with a scraping and a scratching sound. A flagstone slowly slid open in the floor of the cathedral.

And emerging from the dark and dusty hole . . .

Rising slowly from the blackness . . .

A marble coffin carved in the shape of a sleeping lion, his front paws lying crossed upon his chest, his stone mane cascading around his shoulders.

The pilgrim bear gasped aloud.

'BEHOLD! IT IS THE SARCOPHAGUS OF ST STATHAM!'

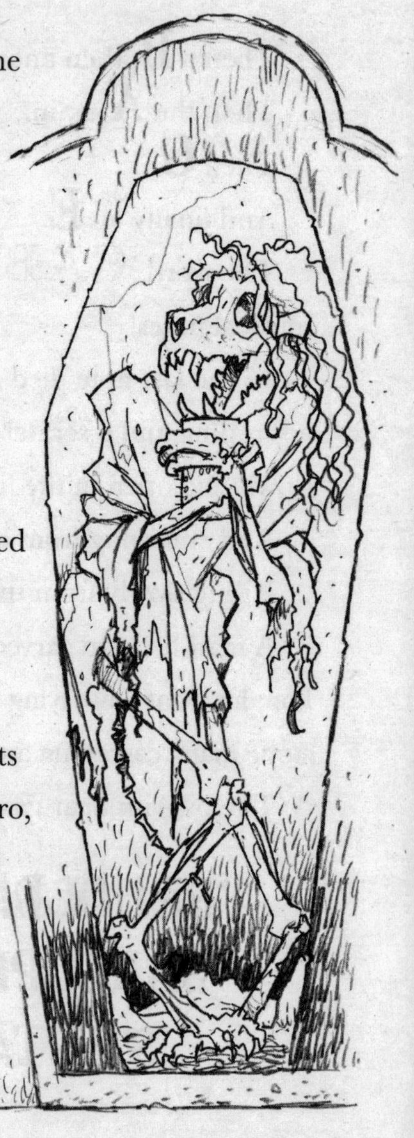

And then the front of the sarcophagus slowly swung open, revealing the dried and crumbling remains of St Statham himself.

And look!

Can you see it?

There!

Clutched in the shrivelled arms of the saintly lion!

A book!

A dusty old notebook! Its title, hastily scribbled in biro, was a single, spidery word:

Doomsday

CHAPTER TWENTY-SEVEN
The Revolution

Some claim that cleanliness is to be admired. I'd warrant this is, in part, true. I myself take an annual bath. Naturally I stay clear of **soap**, for the scent masks my natural musk, which is a source of great conversation wherever I go.

Still, one must also be aware of the virtue of dirt. For without dirt there can be no cleanliness. Without a **dirty hankie**, there can be no **unblocked nose**. Without **dirty knees**, there can be no match-winning ***SLIDING TACKLE***. And without the **stinking sewer** there can be no CLEAN CITY.

And it was from this sewer he came. From a broken grate beside the font, leaning on an ancient cotton bud plucked from the congealed slopes of the underground **FATBERG**.

Findus the rat!

'Down with the Grand Zhool!' he cried. 'Up with the revolution!'

The congregation turned to look at the Grand Zhool. Who dared challenge his rule?

The Grand Zhool moved to face his new challenger and laughed wickedly, his large tombstone teeth clacking together with each booming **ha**!

'More filthy vermin!' The smile died from his snout. 'Kill him.'

And, with those dreadful words, the Fur

Coat of Righteousness sprang into life. Bounding down the aisle towards Findus went a slavering bloodthirsty troop of weasels!

Findus raised the dirty cotton bud above his head and squeaked loudly.

And suddenly the cathedral **swarmed** with rats. A column of furry soldiers raced up from the broken grate.

His comrades.

His colony.

His family.

The weasels met the wave of rats head on in a mass of fur and claws. But still the rats surged forward, like a never-ending wave. The weasels were overwhelmed!

Govvel's eyes darted towards the exit. He licked his lips.

'Your Grace,' he said, 'perhaps it might be prudent to, er, retreat to the palace?'

The Grand Zhool snarled. He turned back to face Mabel, Carruthers and Speke just in time to see Mabel reaching into the coffin and plucking the DOOMSDAY BOOK from the grasp of St Statham.

'You,' he growled. 'It's you who has caused all this. A filthy, stinking **hooman**.'

And he drew a silver dagger from his pocket and stalked towards Mabel Jones.

Mabel raised her cutlass and they circled each other warily.

Then the Grand Zhool attacked!

He was fast, his colossal, rippling bulk moving in the blink of an eye. Mabel's cutlass **bounced harmlessly** off his leathery hide. He grabbed her with one hand and hurled her against the stone coffin, setting the great sarcophagus rocking. The impact knocked the wind from Mabel's lungs and some, if not all, of the hope from her heart.

She gazed up at the Grand Zhool and weakly raised her cutlass.

Taking a handkerchief from his white robes, he hurriedly wiped his hands.

'Filthy creature,' he muttered.

Then he raised the silver dagger high above his head and prepared to stab it deep into the body of Mabel Jones.

'May St Statham have no mercy on your rotten, festering, criminal soul!'

A PAW CAUGHT HIS WRIST!

Speke!

'I say, this is intolerable!' he cried. 'Dash it all! I'm really quite upset.'

For a moment, Speke's trembling muscles strained against the strength of the Grand Zhool.

But no otter is strong enough to grapple with a hippo.

With a sudden jerk, the Grand Zhool stabbed the dagger with as much force as he could muster into Speke's heart.

Speke staggered backwards.

'C-c-cripes!' he stammered.

Then he fell to the floor.

Carruthers knelt by his side, cradling his friend in his arms.

'Timothy. Oh, my Timothy!'

Speke's eyelids fluttered.

'Who is it?' he whispered weakly.

'It is I, Carruthers.'

'Nanny Mimsy?'

Carruthers frowned.

'No, it's CARRUTHERS!'

'Kiss me goodnight, Mimsy, so I shall have sweet dreams . . .'

Carruthers leant forward and kissed his best friend on the forehead.

'Goodnight, sweet Timmy.'

But there was no reply.

Gently he laid his friend's head on the cold stone floor.

The Grand Zhool smiled wickedly.

'Much as I enjoyed that heart-warming death scene, I believe we have unfinished business.'

But, just as he finished making this cruel jibe, the Grand Zhool looked up in horror!

The giant sarcophagus, set rocking by the impact of Mabel Jones, was teetering towards him. The crumbling remains of St Statham leant **precariously** from their final resting place, fixing the Grand Zhool with a hollow-eyed empty-socket stare.

And then the coffin fell forward.

Two tonnes of solid marble.

The Grand Zhool's huge jaw gaped open. He flung his huge flabby arms in front of his face to protect himself, but it was futile.

No beast, not even one of his

tremendous
size,

could survive the **crushing** weight.

The vast stone sarcophagus lay face down on the floor of the cathedral.

St Statham had shown his displeasure.

THE GRAND ZHOOL WAS DEAD.

Mabel shrank away from the grisly sight. Jarvis and Omynus ran down the aisle towards her.

Jarvis ducked as a gunshot ricocheted off a marble pillar behind him and shattered a stained-glass window.

'We need to get out of here!'

Beneath the dome, a battle was raging between the Grand Zhool's soldiers and the angry rats of the **FATBERG**.

Carruthers hauled the fallen form of Speke over his shoulder. Tears were streaming down his furry cheeks.

'Oh, Timmy! You were always my hero!'

And, together, the gang of bruised and battered friends raced from the cathedral.

CHAPTER TWENTY-EIGHT
The Last Words of Sir Timothy Speke

Mabel watched from the stern of the *Sunbeam* as the city of **Otom** disappeared into the distance.

Their mission was complete. The DOOMSDAY BOOK had been recovered. For now, **ALBEMARLE** was safe. And Pelf too. Maybe even the hooman race could be saved. But at what cost? Speke. Poor, dear Speke . . .

Dearest Nanny Mimsy,

If you are reading this, then I have been killed. Please apologize to Mother on my behalf. And please, Nanny Mimsy, dear sweet Nanny Mimsy, dry your sweet and wrinkly eyes. Think not of the talented young otter kit you raised in the nurseries of Speke Towers Country Estate and the exclusive-addressed townhouse we occupied when Mother was on her shopping trips in Crumbridge. Instead, think of Sir Timothy Speke, secret agent, who fought for the noblest of causes. Think of an otter who died defending his country from insidious foreign powers. Think of an otter who would have made his father proud.

I love you, Nanny Mimsy.

God save the Queen!

Timmy x

In the cabin, Professor Carruthers Badger-Badger took a deep breath and pressed Speke's letter to his heart.

He looked at Mabel.

'They say that sadness is just a chemical reaction that occurs within the body. It seems **irrational** that, knowing this, I can't suppress this feeling of hopeless, hopeless gloom . . .' He wiped a tear from his eye. 'This dashed wind!'

Mabel put her hand on his shoulder. She wished she had something to say. Some words that would make everything all right. But she didn't. How could she? There were no words that could.

Carruthers swallowed hard.

'Mabel, Speke's passing leaves me with the blackest of holes in that part of my heart that science can't define. The part that stores my deepest feelings.' He let out a stifled sob. 'Oh, Mabel, he was a true friend. The best friend one could ever wish for.'

He turned his tear-streaked muzzle towards her. And his eyes widened in horror!

'Mabel, **WATCH OUT**!'

A slim wet-lipped gopher had stepped from the shadows.

Govvel.

He was holding the Zhool's dagger, but in his tiny paws it was like a sword. And its sharp end was pressed against the back of Mabel Jones.

'You've ruined everything, hooman. Ten years I spent grovelling to that fat hippopotamus! And finally, just when all those sponge baths had paid off, when I was a somebody, the second most powerful creature in the **holy city of Otom** – you come along!'

Mabel winced as she felt the cold metal against her skin.

'You've ruined everything!'

There was a cough from the floor.

Sir Timothy Speke sat up and shook his head.

'Good morning, Mother,' he said. 'I think I must've fainted!'

He winced, reached into his waistcoat pocket and removed his father's medal. Bent, but not broken, from the thrust of the Grand Zhool's silver dagger.

'My goodness!' He looked around the room at the boggling faces before him. 'Father's medal. It saved my life!'

And, taking advantage of the **distraction**, Mabel Jones slipped from Govvel's grip and leapt round to face him, cutlass in hand.

But this time she wasn't fast enough.

With a hateful grimace, Govvel thrust the blade towards her chest . . .

CHAPTER TWENTY-NINE
The Deadly Schphzzz!

Schphzzz!

CHAPTER THIRTY
The Aftermath of the Deadly Schphzzz!

On my travels I've had many encounters with venomous creatures. I've trodden on the annoyingly well-hidden **slipper toad**, sat on the wrong end of a **cushion cobra** and sucked the venom from a bum punctured by the poisoned spur of a particularly aggressive **platypus**. However, there is none more deadly than the thick and sticky liquid hand-wrung from the warty-skinned venomous amphibian **Herbert's newt**.

Once in your blood it acts fast. As it travels around your body, it causes **spasms**, **constrictions**, **contortions**, **gurning** and seven of the twelve main types of **grimace**. By the time it gets to your heart, all is lost.

In the cabin of the *Sunbeam* time stands still.

Still enough for us to investigate this frozen slice of a nanosecond. Let us dissect this dreadful segment of **impending death**.

Mabel Jones is facing the sunken-faced gopher Govvel.

Govvel stands before her, the Grand Zhool's dagger gripped between both paws and thrusting towards the chest of Mabel Jones.

Sir Timothy Speke sits confused, his father's medal still clutched in his paw.

Carruthers and Jarvis are lunging for Govvel, desperation in their eyes.

Look harder still.

There is the elusive Omynus Hussh, shifty character that he is, paused in the act of rifling through the trouser pockets of the stricken Speke. For what purpose, we don't know – but I'm sure there'll be a **perfectly rational** explanation later.

No one can stop the gopher's deadly blow.

Unless . . .

What was that whispered **Schphzzz!** that zipped through the air like a purposeful wasp?

Take another step back and look.

There, at the door to the cabin, is a small robed figure. The kindly-faced Sister Miriam, on her way home from her **pilgrimage**, one paw tucked inside her handbag.

The pause in time allows us the luxury of peeking inside.

Beneath the usual sundries to be found inside a nun's handbag – the bus tickets, cough drops and emergency tissues – lies a metal tube, a sequence of cogs and a coiled spring.

A clockwork construction capable of firing a small pointed object through the air at great speed.

And look! There at the final **Z** of the **Schphzzz!** it hangs. Heading for the neck of Govvel. Waiting for time to restart.

DO NOT TOUCH IT!

Observe the thick and sticky liquid that drips from its tip. A liquid hand-wrung from the warty-skinned venomous amphibian **Herbert's newt**.

But will this dart and its payload of painful spasming death reach Govvel before he finishes the fatal thrust that will skewer poor young Mabel Jones?

Let us restart time and see.

It does!

It does!

It does!

The blade remains unplunged!

Mabel Jones's heart remains unstabbed!

Mabel Jones is alive!

But Govvel . . . Govvel's eyes open wide in shock and confusion. The dagger falls to the floor. He drops to his knees. His wet lips twist through seven of the twelve main types of contorted **grimace**.

'It can't be,' he utters, his left leg dancing uncontrollably. 'It can't be! I'm too important to die . . . I'm –'

And, with his final sentence unfinished, he falls to the floor.

CHAPTER THIRTY-ONE
The Exciting Final Chapter

Mabel stood up and adjusted her belt.

'Sister Miriam! You saved me!'

Sister Miriam clicked a switch in her handbag. Beneath the toffee wrappers, leaky biros and knitting yarn, the reloading mechanism of her CONCEALED DART GUN activated.

She pointed the handbag at Mabel.

'Yes, I did. A mark of respect from one adventurer to another. You did well, Mabel. Much better than I expected.'

'I don't understand.'

Sister Miriam smiled, and her large and bulging eyes wrinkled kindly.

'Keep your hands well away from your cutlass, please. I like you, Mabel Jones – we ladies have to stick together – but I will kill you if I have to.'

Mabel frowned. The rabbit looked like Sister Miriam, but her voice was different.

She moved differently.

And there was something familiar about her eyes . . .

'The **hedgehog**!' gasped Jarvis. 'The one that tried to kill Mabel. It was you!'

Sister Miriam nodded.

'And the **beggar**. The one who almost got us arrested in **Otom**.'

'Yes, that was me too.'

Carruthers gasped.

'And when you dropped the biscuit tin you *meant* for the Alsatian battlecruiser to hear. You wanted us to get caught!'

Sister Miriam smiled. 'Very true.'

Speke scratched his head.

'But that means you can only be . . . **VON KLAAR**!'

Without taking her bulging eyes from Mabel, the character formerly known as Sister Miriam leant forward and picked up the **DOOMSDAY BOOK** from the cabin table. Then she shook off her wimple and removed her long rabbit ears. Her bulging eyes darted around the room, and a long tongue flicked from her mouth and tasted the air.

SHE WAS A CHAMELEON!

Von Klaar smiled a wide reptilian smile.

'Indeed. I have been one step behind you all along in the hunt for the DOOMSDAY BOOK. But you have brought it to me in the end. Thank you, Mabel Jones. My superiors back in Alsatia will be very grateful to get their hands on this.'

And, with those revealing words, she backed from the cabin and locked the door.

Mabel looked at Jarvis.

Jarvis looked at Mabel.

Carruthers shook his head in disbelief.

'A woman!' he exclaimed.

Out on the deck of the Sunbeam, Von Klaar carefully sealed the DOOMSDAY BOOK in a waterproof bag, took a deep breath and dived gracefully into the sea.

She trod water briefly, watching as the Sunbeam drifted over the horizon.

Then suddenly a periscope appeared. An Alsatian submarine!

Within moments she was aboard.

Another successful mission for the master spy Von Klaar!

She patted the sealed bag that held the DOOMSDAY BOOK – the book that contained the power that would allow Alsatia to defeat **ALBEMARLE** once and for all.

Von Klaar smiled.

It was going to be a lovely war.

The End

I'm sorry to have to break it to you but that actually was *The End*.

Maybe in the storybooks you normally read, a happy ending is guaranteed. Maybe in that make-believe world that's what happens. Not here. The pages you can see after this one – there's no story on those. They're just **blank pages** and the **boring bits** that most books have at the end. Probably just some list of people who have insisted on being thanked.

For this is real life, and in real life not everything always works out OK.

Heroes fail, villains win, and sometimes a long-awaited delivery of pickled onions arrives damaged and the pickling vinegar stains your new carpet.

So the moral of this story?

**REAL LIFE IS HARD,
SO JUST GIVE UP.**

What's that?

You don't accept it?

You **WON'T** accept it?

You don't want to give up?

Well.

You've surprised me. I had you down for a pallid-hearted quitter. A craven-faced splitter. A **coward**, even.

But, no, you've passed the test.

A true unlikely adventurer never accepts an early ending. A true unlikely adventurer will battle to the bitter end, to the very last page. To the very last word. To the final full stop.

Just in case.

Because there are more pages to come. And, while they *may* be blank, or merely contain the boring bits of book that all books are supposed to have, maybe . . .

Just maybe . . .

The story will continue.

So read on, you fool.

Quickly!

Before we miss it.

Where were we?

Ah yes. Aboard the Alsatian submarine.

The commander, a large dog, turned to Von Klaar.

'You have done it again, Von Klaar. The emperor will be very pleased indeed.'

Von Klaar nodded. Things *had* gone rather well.

Almost too well . . .

She gulped, as though she had swallowed a tiny seed of **uncertainty**.

That strange seed planted itself in her stomach, quickly budding into a **little worry** that almost instantly blossomed into a fully grown **sense of dread**.

Something wasn't right.

Carefully, Von Klaar opened the waterproof bag and took out the DOOMSDAY BOOK.

She turned the cover and read the first page.

The Peach
by Sir Timothy Speke

We wandered 'mongst the peach trees,
I smothered her with kisses,
And held her in my paws once more,
Caressed her golden whiskers.

Von Klaar stared in disbelief. Frantically she turned the page.

She told me of Sir Basil Smythe,
The husband she'd forgotten.
I thought I'd picked a juicy fruit;
Alas, the peach was rotten.

The
DOOMSDAY
BOOK
had been switched!

THE END

Outside a tea shop in Crumbridge, an ancient marmoset lecturer mumbles something to a pretty student over afternoon tea. His **fanciful scientific theories** are lost on his young companion, who is distracted by the scone crumbs lodged in the professor's greying whiskers.

Next door, however, behind the inauspicious frontage of **DREARY & SNORES ANTIQUARIAN BOOKS OF MINOR INTERES**, something more dramatic is unfolding.

A group of friends are waiting for a **TOP-SECRET** meeting to begin . . .

Pelf stretched his legs and exhaled a toxic cloud of greeny-brown pipe smog that drifted about his head in a foul-smelling cloud.

'Ah, fresh air! I'm glad to be free of that stuffy prison cell, snuglet.' He rubbed his hairy neck. 'And free of that **noose**. My neck was so constricted I could hardly smoke. Tell me again how you knew to swap the book.'

Mabel smiled.

'It was all thanks to Omynus really. I wish I'd listened to him earlier.'

Omynus Hussh rubbed his head against her leg and looked up at her with his saucery eyes.

'I is very mistrusting,' he said proudly. 'Being from such a wicked background of thieveryness, I knows there was something fishsome about the rabbitty lady. So I went through the otter's

pockets to switch his poetry book for the
DOOMSDAY BOOK.'

Speke slapped his thigh and laughed.

'Well, I'll be!'

Mabel scratched the little loris behind the ears.

All was silent.

Reassuringly silent.

The attractive chicken Springfeather looked up from his typewriter.

'Sir Lockheed will see you now.'

Sir Lockheed Beagle turned the ancient notebook round in his paws and smiled.

'The DOOMSDAY BOOK. Who would've thought that something so unassuming could contain the secret to the destruction of a whole civilization.'

Sir Lockheed lifted a teacup to his muzzle and took a sip. 'You haven't read it yet?'

Carruthers stepped forward.

'As per your instructions, it has remained unopened since its recovery.'

Sir Lockheed nodded.

'Excellent. As you have seen with your own eyes, the world is still on the brink of war. A fleet of **Alsatian battleships** has blocked the sea passage to the Near Far East.' He frowned.

'Tea reserves are running low.'

'Crumbs!' squeaked Speke. 'That *is* serious.'

'In addition, our network of spies informs us that Alsatian troops are gathering on their frontier.'

He looked sternly over the top of his spectacles. 'Things look bleak for **ALBEMARLE** but, thanks to you and your friends, Mabel Jones, we still stand a chance.'

He sat down at his desk and tapped the DOOMSDAY BOOK.

'Because, for all its military might, the **Alsatian Empire** doesn't have this. The secret to the destruction of the hooman race.'

He passed the book to Springfeather.

'If you'd be so kind.'

Springfeather opened the notebook.

He looked at Sir Lockheed. 'The first page is missing.'

'That will be the one that Sir Leopold Guppy stole from St Hilda's Convent,' explained Mabel. 'It's been burnt.'

Springfeather nodded and turned to the next page. He began to read:

'*. . . digital equipment has malfunctioned and I write now with pen on paper, lost deep within this cursed labyrinth, hundreds of metres beneath the ground. The winding tunnels with their traps and trials have taken their toll on our party. Hipkins is dead. Polson is missing. Only I remain to record the doom that we have unleashed upon our own people. For years we've searched for the fabled tomb of Mosp, the god-king of ancient Egypt – guardian of the underworld and bearer of a weapon so terrifying that it could wipe his enemies from the face of the earth.*

'*And then we found it.*

'*We wanted that weapon, for that very same purpose – to rid the world of our enemy. But we did not understand its true nature. For its power was too great for us to control. I saw it. I saw the black fog that enveloped the globe. I saw cities crushed. Our cities, as well as the cities of our enemies.*

'*And now I write this in the hope that one day it will be found and our mistake can somehow be undone. There* is *a way. All you need to do is . . .*'

Springfeather looked up from the book.

'It ends there,' he said. 'Those are the last words ever written by a hooman.'

Mabel looked at Jarvis.

'The weapon they found destroyed everyone on earth!'

Sir Lockheed nodded.

'Now imagine a weapon of such power in the hands of our enemies. What the **Alsatian Empire** might do with it.'

The room fell silent.

Sir Lockheed scratched behind a shaggy ear and looked at the map.

'So where is this **Egypt**?' he muttered.

Mabel walked to the map. The footure world was so different from the world she once knew. Continents had shifted and sunk, and everywhere had different names. But there were still a few clues.

She pointed to an area marked as *The Unknown*.

'I think it's about here.'

Carruthers stepped forward to the map.

'The nearest settlement is the small outpost of **Zinderneuf**.' He smiled. 'It's under **ALBEMARLE** control. We have a small fort there, don't we? Our Foreign Legion has never lost a battle!'

Springfeather looked at Sir Lockheed, his face a picture of grim yet handsome chickenliness.

'Sir, Fort Zinderneuf fell to the **Alsatian army** last week.'

Sir Lockheed frowned. Then he looked at

Mabel and his eyes twinkled.

'Mabel. Someone must go into *The Unknown* and find this secret weapon before it falls into enemy hands. Will you help us in our hour of need?'

Mabel Jones looked at **PELF**.

Then she looked at **JARVIS**.

And then she looked at

Omynus Hussh.

Finally she looked at

SIR LOCKHEED BEAGLE.

'WE ACCEPT!'

digital equipment has malfunctioned
nd I write now with pen and paper.
ost deep within this cursed labyrinth
beneath the ground

I saw it. I saw the black fog that enveloped the globe. I saw cities crush Our cities as well as the cities of our enemies.

ACKNOWLEDGEMENTS

Special thanks to . . .

Paul, my agent.

Ross for his illustrations.

Mandy for the text design.

Everyone at Puffin and Viking, especially **Ben**, **Joanna**, **Tig**, **Laura**, **Jacqui**, **Wendy**, **Sophie** and **Hannah**.

Old friends **Megan** and **Rich W** for helping from afar.

Ellen for listening (or pretending to listen) to my excellent ideas.

But mostly thanks to **you** for taking the time to read this book to the very end.

For the safe disposal of your teachers' biscuits, please send them to:

The Narrator of *The Unlikely Adventures of Mabel Jones*
Room 7c
Pickled Onion Museum
The Footure

COULD YOU SAVE THE HOOMAN RACE?

The fate of the **hooman race** is in your hands . . . What would you do?

You stumble across a chest of stolen treasure . . . What do you do?

A. Share the gold among the poor.

B. Invest in a new pirate ship.

C. Buy a castle. Spend the change on deadly poison.

Which of the seven deadly pirate sins are you most likely to commit?

A. Cake-baking.

B. Mercy.

C. Snitching.

What would be your most prized possession?

A. The finger bones of a long-dead saint.

B. A cutlass.

C. A weapon so powerful it could destroy the world.

When you meet a librarian, do you . . .

A. Borrow a book?

B. Sheath your cutlass (for now)? They may have information that can help you.

C. Unleash the venomous toad you have concealed in your packed lunch box?

On holiday, where are you most likely to be found?

A. Relaxing with a book on the beach.

B. Looking for adventure in the wilds.

C. Sweating in a foreign prison, held on various charges of smuggling.

Mostly A:

Your cowardly ways are commendable, but saving the world requires tough choices to be made. The hooman race is doomed.

Mostly B: It will take more than a combination of brains and bravery to save the world. The hooman race is doomed.

Mostly C:

Have you considered being a politician?

Your story starts here . . .

Do you **love books** and **discovering new stories**?
Then **www.puffin.co.uk**
is the place for you . . .

- Thrilling adventures, fantastic fiction and laugh-out-loud fun
- Brilliant videos featuring your favourite authors and characters
- Exciting competitions, news, activities, the Puffin blog and SO MUCH more . . .

www.puffin.co.uk